Advance praise for *A*

"Fans of contemporary regional mys[...]
further adventures."

"More than just a detective novel, this book is a reflection on the changing landscape of the West and the redemptive power of family. The work of a storyteller at the peak of his form, the return of private investigator Gus Corral reminds me of nothing less than *The Long Goodbye* set in Colorado. Thrilling, heartbreaking and engrossing, *Angels in the Wind* is the best yet from one of the masters of the genre."
—David Heska Wanbli Weiden, author of *Winter Counts*

"What can I say? I absolutely loved *Angels in the Wind: A Mile High Noir*. Manuel Ramos pulls all the right strings in a novel that is at once heart-pounding and tinged with melancholy. Ramos's protagonist, Gus Corral, is a Latino everyman with grit and heart who is forced to reckon with small-town hurt and prejudice. There are not too many authors who can craft a mystery with such depth and complexity. A fantastic read."
—Jon Bassoff, author of *The Lantern Man*

"A labyrinth of misdirection and treachery. Manuel Ramos shoves his very flawed PI, Gus Corral, back into the fray and we cheer as he bulls his way toward justice amid a tangle of family secrets, mayhem and murder."
—Mario Acevedo, co-author of the
high-drama western, *Luther, Wyoming*

"Manuel Ramos is a legend of Chicano noir, and he's done it again with *Angels in the Wind*. Gus Corral is on the case in Melton, Colorado, a small town with some big secrets and characters who might just remind you of a long-lost cousin. In this gripping noir, there's sexy jazz, rolling bluffs, a missing teenager and the weight of history at every turn. Utterly readable and atmospheric, I couldn't put this book down."
—Kali Fajardo-Anstine, author of *Sabrina & Corina*

Praise for the work of Manuel Ramos

"One thing is almost as certain as death and corruption: Manuel Ramos' Chicano angst. You'll find plenty of all three in his jazzy, fast-paced and delirious whodunits, which stand as an unparalleled achievement in American crime literature."
—Ilan Stavans

"Manuel Ramos is one of my all-time favorite authors and in *My Bad* he delivers everything I look for in a noir tale. Gus Corral is the guy I want on my side if I'm in trouble and Ramos proves once again he is the master of creating great characters. Clear your schedule and be prepared to read this blitz attack of noir in one sitting." —Jon Jordan, *Crimespree Magazine* on *My Bad*

"Ramos explores issues of the border, identity, violence and slights from outside the community, as well as within. They are thought-provoking and unpredictable. Many linger long after they end; and often they contain depth charges that explode in the reader's mind after the story has ended. His novels belong on your book shelves." —*Los Angeles Review of Books* on *The Skull of Pancho Villa and Other Stories*

"Ramos puts Latinos back in the picture. He is known as a crime writer, but that doesn't quite capture what he does. His books are love stories, political dramas, mordant cautionary tales. Characters who are Latino, black and white, artists, professionals and laborers, are described in staccato chapters, like a catchy *corrido*." —*Los Angeles Times* on *The Skull of Pancho Villa and Other Stories*

"The Godfather of Chicano noir hits us hard with this collection. Great range, dark visions and lots of mojo—much of it bad to the bone. A fine book!" —Luis Alberto Urrea, author of *Into the Beautiful North*, on *The Skull of Pancho Villa and Other Stories*

"As invigorating as a dip in a Rocky Mountain stream." —*Mystery Scene* on *Desperado: A Mile High Noir*

"A dark mix of North Denver gangsters and Catholicism, but it's [the] setting that really grips readers. Nostalgia is combined with reality . . . Ramos gets it right." —*Denver Post* on *Desperado: A Mile High Noir*

"A very impressive debut." —*Los Angeles Times* on *The Ballad of Rocky Ruiz*

"A thickly atmospheric first novel—with just enough mystery to hold together a powerfully elegiac memoir of the heady early days of Chicano activism." —*Kirkus Reviews* on *The Ballad of Rocky Ruiz*

"Ramos succeeds brilliantly in marrying style and substance to form a seamlessly entertaining novel [with] characters and scenes deeply etched with admirable brevity and skill." —*Publishers Weekly*, starred review, on *Blues for the Buffalo*

ANGELS IN THE WIND

A Mile High Noir

Manuel Ramos

 Arte Público Press
Houston, Texas

Recovering the past, creating the future

Arte Público Press
University of Houston
4902 Gulf Fwy, Bldg 19, Rm 100
Houston, Texas 77204-2004

Cover design by Mora Des!gn

Library of Congress Control Number: 2021930217

♾ The paper used in this publication meets the requirements of the American National Standard for Information Sciences—Permanence of Paper for Printed Library Materials, ANSI Z39.48-1984.

© 2021 by Manuel Ramos
Printed in the United States of America

21 22 23 24   4 3 2 1

This book is dedicated to my brother, Michael Ramos, my brother-in-law, William "Bill" Hurtado, Jr. (QEPD), and la familia de José de Jesus Hernández Diaz (QEPD) and Teodora Castillo Hernández (QEPD), for all your love and support.

Special thanks to Nicolás, Marina, Gabi and all the staff of Arte Público Press.

One

"You ain't from around here, are you?"

The cracked voice wrenched me out of my private fog.

"Depends on what you mean by *around here*." I said the words without thinking about them. I struggled to grasp the moment.

"Melton. This town. Colorado boonies."

He was an older guy, maybe late fifties, but it had taken a hundred years to get there. The first thing I noticed about him was his stained red MAGA cap. The second was his skin. It looked like someone poured brown tar over his head and the tar settled into a shiny topcoat lined with stiff wrinkles and flat black spots. His flannel shirt hung loosely over spotted jeans that hugged a bony frame. Pink fingers, crooked and rough, gripped his beer bottle as though the booze came from the fountain of youth, as though it could change a life. Maybe it had already changed his.

I imagined shouting that my ancestors once roamed the arid landscape that swirled in a dusty haze around the town, centuries before any white man trekked through the sagebrush hoping to stumble onto a city made of gold. For an instant I wanted nothing more than to launch into a lecture about how Melton's city limits sprawled across what had been the border of northern Mexico and that, yes, indeed, when all was said and done, I *was* from *around here.*

"Denver," I said.

He nodded and smiled, proud of himself.

"I knew it. Yessir."

In the past I would have asked how he knew. Or I might have remarked that he'd made a lucky guess, or maybe he'd seen something of Denver in my pickup that leaked oil in the bar's parking lot.

But I didn't do any of that. I didn't care.

"That's a nasty lookin' welt or whatever on your forehead there," he said.

My guts tightened. I didn't want to say anything, but I had to respond. I didn't have a choice. I shrugged, turned and looked directly at him.

"Don't mean to pry," he muttered. He kind of stumbled backwards, only an inch or so, but I noticed. He looked away. "I'm harmless. Curious, yeah. But harmless."

"Got hit with a baseball bat." The words stuck in my dry throat, but he understood.

I paused, worried that again I was saying too much, that the filter I once had for keeping my personal business to myself was broken. Worried that I didn't know how to act, how to maintain, anymore.

He sucked in his breath. "That must'a hurt."

"Unconscious for a day or two," I continued. "Took a while to get back on my feet. Still can't see right, got fucked-up headaches and some days I can't think straight." For the first time I saw that the man's forehead was slick with sweat. "I don't like to talk about it."

I returned to my beer.

The sign outside said SAND CREEK SALOON. Inside, a half-dozen gray and grizzled men in overalls and wrecked boots did their best to live up, or down, to all that the bar's name implied. They had to know the history of the 1864 Sand Creek Massacre, didn't they? I was sure none of them were Cheyenne or Arapaho. Even if they knew about Colonel John Chivington, the Third Colorado Cavalry, and the killing of more than a hundred unarmed women and children, they wouldn't care.

"Uh, sorry to hear that," the man mumbled. "Baseball's a dangerous game, yessir."

I almost corrected him. My bashed-in head had nothing to do with a game.

He picked up his beer, turned away and made like he saw someone he knew. He shuffled to the corner where an old-fashioned juke box played a mournful country boy trying to imitate Willie Nelson. The singer couldn't pull it off.

The curious man didn't want to learn anything else about the beat-up Chicano who was out-of-place in the weathered beer joint and who told sketchy stories of baseball bats and headaches while he nursed a Bud Light.

On second thought, I wasn't out-of-place.

"Agustín?"

It took a second for me to respond. Then another tick of the clock to recognize Essie Montoya, the reason I was in the saloon, and why I'd taken my headaches and lost focus to dusty Eastern Colorado.

"Hello, Essie. It's been awhile."

She reached across the space between us and gave me a hug. From my bar stool I awkwardly returned the affectionate greeting. Her body gave off heat from the late summer day outside.

"Good to see you, cuz," she said. "I wasn't sure you'd show up."

I hadn't been a hundred percent sure about that either. My older sister made the arrangements, explained all that Essie needed to know about me and argued for me to take the job. I'd agreed when Essie finally called me. Corrine packed my clothes and toothbrush, shoved me in my truck and waved me on my way.

"Not every day I get a call from a relative I haven't seen for years, and then for that relative to ask about hiring me for a job. I told you I'd be here."

She sat down on the bar stool next to me and wiped her face with a bandana she dug out of her jeans.

"Hot out there, ain't it?" I said.

"Yeah, especially when you walk into town." She stuffed the bandana back into her jeans. "And here you are. Agustín Corral. In the flesh. Just like you promised on the phone."

"Gus, please. Not used to Agustín."

"Man, that triggers the memories. When you and your sisters visited us, when we lived in Pueblo, you were Gus. You hated the name Agustín. We were all just kids." She shook her head as though it was impossible that we were those children. "Seems like a long time ago."

Essie was related to me on my mother's side of the family in some weird, complicated Mexican way that had been explained to me, more than once, by my mother and then by Corrine. I never quite grasped the connection. Essie, short for Esmeralda, was my "cousin" and I left it at that. I hadn't seen her since my mother's funeral, years ago. When she called me at my office and said she and her brother wanted to hire me, I said yes without giving it too much thought, especially with Corrine's pressure. Not only was she family, but I was in bad shape from the beating I'd suffered at the hands of my infamous baseball client. I was tired, sore and disoriented. I wanted out of overcrowded Denver. I had to get away from the city's too-hip art and restaurant districts, noisy craft beer joints, an overpriced lifestyle and the raspy, dying gasps of the hometown I'd once known. Goodbye, Cow Town. Hello . . . what? Denver was mutating and I didn't want to be a witness. I couldn't get anything done, which meant I couldn't make money. Maybe I was through as an investigator. I was a stranger in the only city where I'd ever lived, and I didn't like the feeling.

The sparse and monotonous plains of Eastern Colorado offered a destination where I might find my bearings. No distractions, no stress. My only obligation would be to do the job, whatever it was, for my relatives. When that was finished, I could move on or stay put. By then, I figured, I'd have it together again. I'd be my old self.

That's what I tried to convince myself of during the four-hour drive from Denver to Melton and the Sand Creek Saloon, where Essie said we should meet.

"Strange place for a business meeting. Or a reunion," I said.

"Yeah, I know. But it's always open, which is rare in Melton. And George works down the street. He'll be here soon. Hope this is okay."

"You live close?"

"About three miles out of town." She shrugged thin shoulders and gave me a twisted grin as if she were going to say something silly. "Guess I'm stuck here, with my mother."

Corrine told me that Essie made a living as a bookkeeper for various ranchers and other Melton businesspeople. She also did taxes and helped with applying for licenses and permits. There wasn't much of an economy in Melton, or for a hundred miles around, but Essie apparently had a finger on most of what little commerce did exist.

Essie had cared for her mother since she was in high school. Felisa Montoya was a half-blind, sometimes wheelchair-bound woman that Corrine described as a hell-raiser when she was younger, all "piss and vinegar."

"And your brother?"

"For sure he's not going anywhere. Part owner of the shop, raising two kids, and he's on the Town Council. He thinks Melton is perfect."

George had left Melton once, when he joined the Army and did his duty in Afghanistan. I always thought he would ditch the small town for the city, but it hadn't played out that way.

"Well, not quite perfect. Right?"

She nodded. "We wouldn't need you if it was."

"Who's the old guy by the jukebox? Looks like the cat dragged him around for a day or two."

She turned her head in the direction of the twangy music and smiled, then frowned. "That's Werm. Melton's town joker. Harmless. Kooky, but harmless."

"Worm?"

She laughed. "*Werm.* W-E-R-M. I don't even notice the name anymore. His real name's Wermer Wilson Tanney. The Tanneys have lived in these parts since Colorado became a state. Poor Wermer . . . he's been Werm since his momma brought him home from the hospital in Lamar. The family has money, but you wouldn't know it talking to him."

She looked past me and smiled.

A thick hand grabbed my shoulder and spun my bar stool.

"Gus. Long time, cuz."

George Montoya grinned as his fingers dug into my bicep. His oil-stained coveralls covered a lanky, tall frame. He had the same thin body shape and pale skin as his sister. Same golden-brown eyes, same thick, black hair that curled into a ponytail. Same farm kid look. Sunburned, dusty, hard-working.

But the closer I looked, the more I could tell that George was not a well man. His brown eyes were bloodshot and framed with dark circles and wrinkles. The black hair had gray streaks, making him look old and tired, although he wasn't that much older than me.

I stood up from the bar stool and gave him a proper *abrazo*— a family hug. We talked and smiled self-consciously. Then George motioned with his head towards a booth and Essie and I followed his lead.

"A private eye, eh?" George asked. "An investigator. How'd you get into that? Last I heard you were working for a lawyer, like a paralegal. I always thought you'd end up as a lawyer, or a teacher. You talked a lot as a little kid."

Essie and George laughed, and I smiled the best I could. Usually it was Corrine who reminded me that I hadn't lived up to expectations.

For the next ten minutes I relived my recent history, from my release from prison until the day my baseball client killed his brother and almost finished me off. As I talked, I saw in their faces and eyes that, again, I said too much. I couldn't stop. I tried to lighten the mood by explaining that the best thing about prison had been books. I read hundreds of books, I said. My vocabulary had improved, my perspective about the world had changed. I learned about the world beyond the limits of Denver's Northside, where I was born and grew up. Hell, I made prison sound like the best thing short of a college education. When I saw that they weren't impressed, I let my story roll out without considering what impact my words might have. I talked about the ice-fishing caper with the Mexican cop and the shoot-out in the mountains. I went deep, too deep, into my Cuban disaster and the bloody night when the baseball star pounded justice and revenge into his disloyal brother and whacked me dizzy just for being in the way.

Next, I brought them up to speed on how my sisters were doing. Corrine was as political and radical and troublemaking as ever, Maxine still in the music business but settled down with her wife, Sandra. I assured them that Corrine and Max were in better shape than I. Not a high bar, but it was something. I realized too late that they didn't want to hear that.

"You okay now?" Essie asked. She tentatively reached out and placed her hand on my shoulder. "Maybe you should just kick back. Take a vacation."

"Tell you the truth," I answered, "I'm not a hundred percent. Maybe seventy-five. I take painkillers for headaches and something stronger for my mental state. But doing some work out here, away from Denver, it'll do me good. And I want to help with whatever you're dealing with."

Essie looked at George. He nodded.

"Actually," she said. "Corrine suggested we talk with you. I was in Denver a few weeks ago and I stopped by her house. When I told her what was going on, she said she thought you could help us. She did say you were still recovering, but she also said she had no doubt that you were up to it. I talked it over with George. And here we are."

When Corrine said she'd volunteered me for a job, I protested for a minute. I wasn't as sure as my sister about whether I could handle basic life, much less an actual job. Corrine and I eventually

agreed that I should get out of Denver. And she gave me background about our country cousins.

"Hey, Montoya. You want anything to drink? Or eat?" The bartender hollered at us from across the room.

"Gus?" George asked. "They got good burgers here."

I hadn't eaten since I'd scarfed a doughnut during rush hour as
I maneuvered out of the Northside and merged onto I-70 East.

"Yeah, sure. Burger sounds good."

George shouted back at the bartender. "Three burgers and two
Cokes and another beer." He paused. "And cook them good,
Freddy. Last time the burger mooed when I bit into it. No blood on
the plate."

"Yeah, up yours, Montoya," the bartender answered.

Everyone was all smiles, so I assumed an inside joke had played
out in front of me. Maybe it was a ritual whose origins dated back
years.

"Corrine told me a little bit about the trouble with your son,"
I said. "What's going on?"

He looked down at his lap and shook his head. "Yeah, Matías.
Mat."

He raised his head. No more joking. His eyes dulled in the hazy
light of the bar and for an instant I expected tears to glide down his
face. I understood why he looked used up.

"He's run off again. He's done that before, but he's always come
back in a few days, a week at the most. He's a good kid, but he's got
issues. A lot of kids do these days."

His voice was shaky as he talked, and it was easy to see the
stress caused by the fact that he needed to explain his missing son.

"He's a good kid," Essie said. "We all know that. The whole
town knows that. This past year has been different, though. He
wasn't running away last year. This time he's been gone too long…
" Her voice trailed off.

"He's been gone for a month," George said. "Alicia . . . my
daughter Alicia?" I nodded. "Alicia and me . . . we don't know what

to do. We've talked with his friends, the people at the ranch where he was working for the summer, everyone who knows him. Nothing. Nobody knows nothing. Or at least they're not telling us."

Corrine had described Matías Montoya as "a troubled boy." She'd explained that George and his wife, Cindy, adopted him when he was about three. "He's been in trouble with school and the cops," she said. "Especially after Cindy died. Nothing serious, but George must've had his hands full. I wouldn't be surprised if Mat's gone for good this time."

"If he's on the road, I doubt I'll find him," I said to Corrine. "He could be in Mexico by now. Teen-aged runaways usually aren't found unless they want to be found. And I'll be getting a late start."

"But maybe you can find out something to give George a little hope," Corrine said. "Or some relief. Essie said her brother's a mess. If he knows the kid is alive, that might be enough."

And what if he's dead? I thought.

"Can you help?" Essie asked.

Her question jerked me back to Melton and the Sand Creek Bar. "I'll do what I can," I said. "You reported him missing to the police?"

"Sure," George said. "When he'd been gone for a week. The local Chief here, a guy named Rob López, sent out bulletins to other police departments, talked to some of Mat's friends, stuff like that. I guess Mat is in a national database of missing kids. But López can only do so much. He's the one real cop we have, and he's part-time. His help, the guys he calls deputies, are volunteers. Freddy, the bartender, is one. It's not like López set up search parties or anything like that."

"How did Mat manage when he took off before?" I asked. "Does he have a credit card or . . . ?"

"No," George said. "He usually has money from work. He's worked at odd jobs since he was twelve. Now he's a regular on Leroy Bannon's ranch. Mat carries around a lot of cash. I've told him to put it in the bank, but he's stubborn. A couple of times, when he did run out of money and couldn't get back home, he called, and I picked him up. I haven't got that call this time."

The bartender brought us three greasy hamburgers with greasy potato chips. He made a second trip with our drinks. My hunger had peaked, and I swallowed the burger in four bites. I finished off my first beer before I restarted the conversation.

"I'll talk to some of the same people you already talked to," I said. "See if anything pops out. Alicia can help, I assume. She knows his friends, where he used to hang out. And, uh, maybe . . ."

"Maybe she will tell you things about Mat that she wouldn't tell her father, or me?" Essie asked.

"It's possible. Teenagers, you know. Anyhow, I'll do what I can. But, well the truth is that if he doesn't want to come home, there's not much anyone can do. What is he, seventeen?"

"Yeah," George said. "But he looks older and he tries to act older. He's always been bigger than the other kids his age. But he's still a minor. He has to come home if I say so, right?"

A flash of hope in his eyes briefly outshone the worry lines on his forehead.

Essie answered for me. "Not really, George. He can claim to be emancipated, live on his own. He can even make it legal."

"Why would he not want to come home? I don't get it."

"Were you two okay?" I asked. "I mean between the two of you. Fathers and sons don't always get along. Were you arguing about something, maybe he thought you were too strict or . . . ?"

"No, nothing like that," George insisted. He pushed away his plate and stuck a toothpick between his teeth. Almost immediately he spit out the toothpick to continue talking. "I understand he's a young man, not a boy. That's how I treat him. Man to man. I don't impose rules or curfews or anything like that. He has his responsibilities, his chores, work around the house, sure. But that's it. He's self-sufficient, independent, probably too much, and that's my fault. And yet, every time he ran away before, he didn't have a reason. He just had to get away, he would say. We'd argue, both get pissed, but it didn't last. That's why I don't understand. My own son, and I don't understand him."

"Nothing new about that George," I said. "My father didn't understand me. I'd bet yours was the same with you."

At the back of my muddled brain I remembered that when I was seventeen, I believed I had to get away, without reason, without logic. Just go, man, go. It wouldn't have surprised me if someone had said that it was in our family blood, even though Matías Montoya was adopted. Maybe all the Corrals and Montoyas were nothing but troubled runaways, searching for something we couldn't describe, yearning for something we weren't sure existed.

If that were true, God would have to help George Montoya and his son find their own peace because there would be nothing I could do.

Two

When we finished our lunch, George offered photos of Mat and a list of names and addresses of Mat's friends. Essie rode with me as I followed George's van to his house.

A couple of times she started a sentence, but she dropped it quickly.

"There something you want to say?" I finally asked. "You nervous about anything?"

"You're going to think I'm silly," she said.

"I doubt that."

"I like your truck. See, it's silly. But it looks great, inside and out. Don't know if you plan to paint it, but I'd leave it the way it is if it were mine. I love old trucks, especially Apaches."

I'd driven to Melton in my sixty-year-old Chevy, the truck I'd inherited from my father, which meant neither Corrine nor Max wanted it. The truck sat in the backyard of my parents' house for as long as I could remember. I had dim memories of my father crawling under the machine to work on it. Those events were always accompanied with cussing and an angry toss or two of a wrench or pliers. The bruised pickup's odometer was stuck on one hundred fifty-eight thousand hard miles. A washed-out gray-green patina dressed up several dents and scratches. A month after I was released from the hospital, Corrine said I had to move it from the backyard or she would donate it to KUVO, the public radio jazz station.

After I got it running, and bought plates and insurance, I replaced the driver side door—Corrine had pointed out that the gash in the center was dangerous. That explained the conspicuous door coated with black primer. I told anyone who asked that the plan was to paint the truck a sexy candy apple red. They either laughed or accused me of daydreaming. No one believed me.

Even so, the truck had rat rod class. Corrine forced me to take on the pickup's restoration as part of my therapy while I recovered from my bat injury. She figured I needed something to focus on that would help push me back to my old self.

I'd done a few things to the interior: upholstery from a Mexican blanket I found in my ex-wife's second-hand shop, refinished dashboard with new chrome knobs, a plush headliner and carpet on the floor.

A mechanic friend of Corrine's checked out the engine. He did what he could to make sure the truck wouldn't belch smoke or flame out on the freeway as I rushed to serve a restraining order on a client's deadbeat baby daddy. The final touch came courtesy of my artistic sister Maxine. In the center of the black door she'd painted a logo that announced to anyone who cared to look that Agustín "Gus" Corral was a private investigator, LLC. Max included a mystical Aztec/Maya/steampunk graphic that looked vaguely like an eyeball. Gus Corral—the private eye. Who'd ah thought?

Essie and I talked about salvaged pickups and rusty jalopies as I tried to keep up with George. A foxtail of dust from the van enveloped us as soon as we left Melton's main street. After a few minutes of back road speeding and eating George's dust we were at his house.

I parked on the gravel edge of a neat but sparse front yard whose landscape consisted of rocks and cactus.

"Yeah, I'm loving Old Smokey," Essie said.

"My truck doesn't smoke," I said.

"I know, I know, I'm joking," she laughed. She jumped out of the cab and squinted in the sunshine. "But it looks like it should smoke, like it could explode any minute now."

She waved at a group of men across the street who stood around the open engine compartment of a flatbed truck. When they waved back she hurried into the house.

The men stared as I climbed out of my truck. I assumed they were having a meeting, and the thought crossed my mind that I should learn what the meeting was about. A vague feeling of distrust crept up my spine, and I needed to know what they were doing. My fingers began to shake. I sucked in a deep breath and tried to believe that what I felt was nothing but lingering paranoia from my head bashing. The men were most likely friends and relatives doing what friends and relatives do: catching-up, telling jokes, talking about work, swearing at the news. In other words, just guys doing guy things. But it was the middle of the day. Why weren't they at their jobs?

I let it go.

A pair of barking dogs ran from the back of the house. They looked mean and hungry. One was a large, black mongrel with bright teeth, the other a brown collie-looking mutt. They were on a beeline for me when Essie shouted, "Chuy! Coco! Here boys! Over here!" The dogs turned and greeted Essie with more barking until she petted each one. Just like that, they calmed down and threw themselves on the porch floor.

George and Alicia waited in the front room of their small home. An American flag hung in a corner. A bolt action Winchester rested on a rack in another corner. A box of 30-06 bullets was stashed behind the rack. I was surprised that the rifle and ammunition were out in the open until I reminded myself that I was in rural Colorado where everyone owned at least one dog and one gun, and pets and rifles weren't locked up. Next to the rifle was a snapshot of George holding the weapon and standing over a dead deer. Several photographs of a dark-haired woman were scattered around the house, on walls and shelves. There was one framed eight-by-ten of a younger, healthier George in a soldier's dress uniform. I smelled coffee, chile powder and fried beans.

Alicia Montoya stood as tall as her father, but that was the only resemblance. Her dark skin contrasted sharply with his *güero* light complexion. Her face was round and filled in; George had angles and creases. *She must be adopted, too,* I thought.

She stepped forward and introduced herself. She hugged Essie, then sat down. I calculated she was about fifteen years old.

"Alicia can connect you to Mat's friends," George said.

"You should talk with his best friend, Connor Darby." Alicia said. "He's working today."

"Leroy Bannon's place?" Essie asked.

Alicia nodded.

"Yeah, of course," George said.

"After you get settled in," Essie said, "we thought you could stay at my house. More room than with these two." She pointed at George and Alicia.

"Whatever," I said. "I don't have much. A backpack with basics. I can sleep in that motel at the edge of town. I don't want to get in the way."

"Hey, cuz," George said, "you're working for me. And you're family. We'll take care of you. No motel. Essie and Mom's place is big, comfortable. You'll be okay there."

I shrugged. "If that's what you want."

"You want to go to the house first?" Essie asked. "Rest up from the drive?"

I hadn't rested in weeks. It didn't seem likely to happen right then. "I'm okay. We might as well get started."

"We can drive to Bannon's, then later to my house," Essie said. "You have the time *now,* Alicia?"

The girl nodded. She hadn't said much.

"You coming, George?" I asked.

"Uh, I guess so," he answered. "Can't stay long, though. Too much work at the shop." He picked up a pile of photographs and a thin book. "These are the pictures of Mat. His high school yearbook, a few from my phone."

I took the stack from George and thumbed through the photos. Mat was a handsome teenager. Shoulder-length hair, muscular arms, big smile. And, as with Alicia, he looked nothing like George.

≫ ≫ ≫

On the way to the Bannon ranch, I asked Essie a question that had bothered me since we'd had our hamburger lunch. "George seems to be dealing with his son's running away. I mean, he's handling it, not overreacting. You agree with that?"

"You think he should be more upset, more worried?"

"I wouldn't say he *should* be, but to tell you the truth, you seem to be more uptight about Mat than George is. You know George a hell of a lot better than I do. So, I may be missing something here. I didn't remember what you and George looked like until I saw you two in the bar."

"Sure, I get it."

"I have to ask these kinds of questions, part of the job. That's all I'm doing."

She sucked in a deep breath. "The thing about George is . . . he's such a guy. He doesn't show what he's feeling or thinking. He's got one expression, one mood, one attitude. He's been like that since he was a kid, and when he came back from Afghanistan, he'd doubled down on his lack of emotion. He's talked with a doctor from the VA about it."

She could've been describing me, I thought.

"But Mat's disappearance is eating him up. He's not sleeping, he's taking more meds for anxiety, depression. He's talked to me, several times, in panic mode. He's really worried, and I think he's at the point where he can think only the worst about Mat. Of course, he won't show that to anyone except me. He's a very private man. He holds everything inside. You're his last hope, Gus. He's counting on you to find Mat, or to at least find out where he is. He's hoping you'll provide the happy ending."

≫ ≫ ≫

Leroy Bannon limped across the hard dirt driveway that led up to his expensive-looking house. Essie's broad smile hinted that meeting with the rancher was a special occasion. The long hug between the two reinforced my hunch.

Bannon fit my idea of a cowboy. Tall, dressed in faded jeans, a well-worn broad-brimmed hat on his sweaty head, red splotches from the sun across the bridge of his nose. His solid grip when he shook my hand came as no surprise. He listened closely as Essie explained that I was now involved in the search for Mat. He interrupted before George could add anything.

"Like I told Essie and George before, I'm worried about that boy. I don't feel good about any of this."

"Why's that?" I asked.

"Well . . . he's run off before. But not like this time. I think he's trying to really leave."

"What's he running from?"

"I don't want to start trouble, but George will agree they have a strained relationship." He paused, then continued when George didn't respond. "Mat complained about George . . . sorry, but you know it's the truth." Again, George didn't say anything. Bannon wrinkled his face, then went on. "He complained about school, probably about working here, too."

"God, Leroy," Essie said. "George and Mat . . . it's not as bad as you make it sound. No worse than any other parent with a teen-aged boy. Mat's not a complainer. He's actually kind of laid back."

"Yeah, maybe," Bannon said. "Around you."

George patted me on my back. "I gotta get back to work, Gus. I'll see you later. You can fill me in on what you find out, if anything." Without another word, he rushed off.

"Thanks, Leroy," Essie said. "Now I'll have to put up with a hurt and sulking George for another week."

Bannon shrugged. "Look. All I'm saying is that Mat runs off, no secret. I didn't mean to upset George. But I am concerned about the boy. He's always come book in a few days. Sometimes for his pay. I owe Mat a week's wages. Ain't heard a peep from him. Another thing. He knows it's getting critical for work. We got to get the ranch ready for fall, which around here means winter. The house needs work, mostly the roof. There's a mile of fence needs repair. The barn needs cleaning and painting. There's too much to do. Busy time of year. He wouldn't leave us in the lurch like this. At least, he never did before. He's been dependable, everyone knows that. He can be headstrong, rowdy. But he's a good boy, basically."

"That's right," Essie said. There was a hint of irritation in her words.

"Where does he go?" I asked. "He have a favorite place or people he'd go see? You checked with anybody like that, right?"

"I never asked," he said. "Didn't think I should pry into his family stuff."

"It was different places and people," Essie said. "A few times he ended up in Pueblo, once he made it to Denver, and another time he landed in Albuquerque. I think we talked to everyone who might know something."

"Well, except for . . ." Alicia said, ". . . you know, Wes"

Essie frowned. "That guy? He's a waste of time."

Before I could find out more about Wes, Alicia pointed to the barn. "There's Connor," she said. "You should talk with him." She waved at a short red-haired boy who slapped dust out of his jeans and shirt.

This time, Alicia explained who I was and what I was doing. The kid wasn't impressed.

"I told you everything, Alicia. The last time we talked." Connor spoke without anyone asking him any questions. It was obvious he wanted to get away from Mat's relatives and their detective. "Mat's okay. He's just tired of this town and, uh, uh, the people who live here. He's okay. I know it."

"You don't know that, Connor," Alicia said. "Unless you've heard from him since we talked?"

"No, no. I haven't. But he's all right. Mat's like that."

"Like what, Connor?" I asked.

The kid wouldn't look at me. "I don't want to get him in trouble," he mumbled.

"He's already there," I said. I had to try something to get him to open up. "Missing for a month, when you're only seventeen? That sounds like trouble to me. If you were gone for a month, don't you think that would mean trouble for you? Wouldn't you want your family to look for you if you were missing?"

He finally turned his eyes on me. "I ain't Mat. I don't do the things he does. We're friends, that's all. And I'm telling you that he's okay. He has to be."

I moved up close to Connor, standing between them, and tried to hold his attention. I didn't want Alicia or Essie to ask him anything else. I stood between them and Connor.

"You sound pretty sure. You certain he hasn't contacted you? A text, maybe? Or maybe you helped him plan whatever it is he's doing? Maybe you know exactly where he is now? Is that it, Connor? Is that why you're so sure that he's okay? Tell us what you know so we can help him."

The kid's sunburned face wrinkled into a tight mask. "I told you, I don't know where he is. I'm not lying. But, with Mat . . . you must understand . . . he's always talking about going someplace else. He hates it here. Drives him crazy, he says. He's gone, and I don't think he's coming back. I really don't. Alicia . . . you know it, too. Just stop. He's okay. I know he is."

Was the kid trying to convince us or himself? Before I could test the strength of his convictions about the well-being of his friend, he shuddered, almost a full body tremor. Tears rolled out of his eyes, streaking his dust-covered cheeks. Alicia grabbed him, and he leaned into her for support. She held him up, and I saw that she was crying, too.

Three

The weepy teenagers didn't give me anything new. Connor switched between anger and despair, but he didn't know his missing friend's whereabouts. Alicia asked him, repeatedly, about the last messages Mat had sent him. I guess she hoped Connor was holding back and that if she asked him enough times he would spill the beans, and everything would be okay with Mat.

Connor showed us the texts that simply said "later" or "I'll let you know where I am when I know where that is." That's all he had.

"Why the tears?" I asked. "You're afraid of something. Or you think something's happened to Mat. What is it?"

Alicia and Connor shook their heads.

"No, I don't know anything else," Connor said. "It's just that he's never been gone this long. He usually texts me every day. But I haven't heard from him for weeks. We were gonna go to Denver, together, for a weekend. That's the plans we had. Then, he just leaves. Without me. Without a word to Alicia or me. I don't get it."

"There's no one else Mat might've talked to about his leaving?" I asked. "Only you two?"

"Just Wes," Connor said.

"Yes, but . . ." Alicia muttered.

"What? Wes who?"

"They mean Wes Delgado," Essie said. "He doesn't know anything about Mat."

"You should talk to him," Alicia said. "Mat and Wes were friends."

"That's news to me," Essie said.

Alicia and Connor wouldn't look at her.

"Where can I find this Delgado?" I asked. "And what's his story?"

20

"His trailer, what he calls his cabin, is about five miles east of here, on County Road Eight." Essie pointed towards Kansas as she spoke. "He moved here two years ago, said he was a writer, working on a novel. I've never seen *anything* he's written. Not sure he actually writes anything to tell you the truth."

"Why don't you like him, Essie?" I said. "What's your problem with him?"

Essie looked embarrassed for a second, then she shook her head. "When he first showed up, I liked him, and so did everyone else. He can be charming, and he was friendly. He seemed to be serious about writing a book about Colorado and the people of Melton. He talked about books like *Plainsong* and *The Milagro Beanfield War,* said he wanted to write novels like those, about real people, with real drama. Those were his words. He said that a lot. We all supported him, gave him stories, told him the legends and history of Melton and the eastern plains. Some of us gave him more."

She paused, and again I sensed embarrassment. "I started to have my doubts about him when he began borrowing money. Money that he hasn't paid back. He lives like a bum, no job, nothing. As far as I'm concerned, he's a fake, a con man. It's not good that Mat and he were friends. I can't see why they would be."

She wiped her hands across the front of her faded work shirt. "Now, I'm more worried than ever about Mat."

I wrapped up my questioning of Alicia and Connor and concluded I should follow what people were giving me. That meant talking to the Wes Delgado character as soon as I could. Connor agreed to give Essie and Alicia a ride home. Essie protested and said she should go with me, but I reminded her that I was the investigator and that she had to let me do my job. She reluctantly agreed, but only after I asked her to call Delgado so that he would be expecting me, and to make sure that he was at his house.

"House trailer," Essie corrected me. "It's an old Airstream he towed from some place in Oklahoma. He found it online, he said. He lives like a lost soul, but it's more for show than anything else."

"What does that mean?" I asked.

"Oh . . . nothing. I just don't like the man."

A sliver of pain sliced through my head. I felt uneasy, uptight, and I had to get away from the group.

Essie's directions to Delgado's trailer were clear and simple. Follow the road we'd taken to the Bannon ranch for three more miles. Turn off at the sign pointing to the Dead Snake Bluffs. Another mile and a half and she assured me I'd see the shining Airstream up against one of the bluffs. In Denver I would have simply relied on my phone's GPS. Essie cautioned me that Melton's phone service could be sketchy, and almost everyone had a GPS story that ended with someone lost or nowhere near where they wanted to be.

She also warned me that sunset was less than an hour away. "You'll be in the dark on your way back. If you get lost, we might not get your call. And the weather this time of year is a gamble."

"It can rain, hail, even a tornado," Alicia added. "It's the monsoon. One of us should go with you."

"I'm good. I'll be okay. See you all later."

I walked clumsily to my pickup but caught myself before I fell. I was sure they had seen me and were probably shaking their heads, questioning their decision to hire me. I came off as angry, rude, impatient. I considered apologizing, then let it go.

Just my head, I thought. *They'll have to understand.*

Connor and Alicia stood shoulder-to-shoulder while Essie pointed her finger and appeared to lecture them. I waved at them as I drove away. They must not have seen me since they didn't wave back.

➳ ➳ ➳

The trailer was right where Essie said it would be. The bluffs were steep ridges of earth and rock lined up along what must have once been a river. Now it was dry, cracked soil with weeds and boulders.

In front of the Airstream, among pieces of rusty machinery, wooden boxes and worn out tires, a man about my age sat on a lawn chair. He was dressed in a gray T-shirt and jeans. He smoked a cigarette and drank from a can of tomato juice. His gray-brown hair sat on his head in a top knot that would have looked almost hip in Brooklyn. He stared at my truck as I pulled up and killed the engine.

I climbed out of the cab and immediately heard music—slow, sexy jazz. Several wooden box speakers loosely hung on wires strung across the roof line of the trailer.

A pile of rags and pieces of wood stirred as I approached. A brown dog emerged from the pile, stretched his back and leisurely sniffed at my shoes. The guy in the lawn chair stood up.

"You lost?" he said. He dropped his cigarette and crushed it with his shoe.

"You Wes Delgado?"

He slapped his hands together. "You're out here and you know my name. You're already a step ahead of me. What can I do for you?"

"My name's Gus Corral. George Montoya hired me to look for his son, Matías. I'm an investigator."

"No shit? Thought investigators existed only in the movies, or cheap paperbacks. But here you are, eh? Looking for Mat? And you want to talk with me?"

"Hope I'm not bothering you," I said. "Essie was gonna call you, let you know I was coming."

"Yeah, she called."

He didn't explain why he acted surprised when I drove up. "I've been told you were friends with Mat. Maybe you can help with my search."

Wes Delgado dressed like the bum Essie had described. Grease stained the front of his T-shirt. His jeans were ripped, his ancient Reeboks flopped on sockless feet. He looked down-and-out and he lived on his own private junkyard. All in all, he sported a classic wasted hobo look . . . maybe too classic?

I decided within a few minutes of meeting him that Wes Delgado had more than one layer. The vibe I picked up wasn't only that of a burned-out derelict.

He walked to a Styrofoam cooler and fished out another can of tomato juice. "You want one?"

"No thanks. But I could use some water."

He reached into the cooler again and brought out a plastic bottle of water. He tossed it to me.

"I told George and the cop, López, everything I know about Mat's disappearance. It's not much." He sounded sincere but futile, like he wanted to help but doubted that he really could.

"Thanks for doing that," I said. "I'm a pair of fresh eyes. Maybe talking with me you'll trigger something you'd forgotten, or didn't think was important . . . or maybe I'll think of something that those who are too close to Mat wouldn't notice. Maybe. It's a crap shoot, but it's all to help find a missing boy. You'll help with that, right?"

He gave me a half-smile. "Sure, why not? But, before we get to it, you got some I.D.?"

I showed him my laminated PI license and my driver's license, both of which he glanced at quickly without really looking at them. Then we talked.

I learned that Wes Delgado was originally from Chacon, a village in northern New Mexico, and that he'd graduated from New Mexico State with a B.A. in political science. He confirmed that he was a writer and that he hoped to finish his novel in a few months. He offered to show me his manuscript, but I stopped him before we went down that road.

"How about Mat?" I asked. "What's your connection to him?"

He stood up from his broken chair and paced in a small circle in and around the junk in front of his trailer. He kept talking.

"Mat's a smart boy. Too smart for Melton, too smart for his father. The boy has plans, ideas, that he wants to get on with. He and I met when I talked to his English class about writing. He looked me up and wanted to learn all he could about publishing, writing a book, getting ideas, the process. That kind of stuff, you know? He showed me some poetry he'd written. It blew me away. The kid can write. Better than me, I must admit. So, yeah, we became friends. Not everybody liked that, but Mat's the kind of kid who wants to learn shit, find out everything he can, see new places, meet new people. That's not a character trait that the people of Melton can appreciate."

"You knew he was leaving?"

"In a way." He shut up, quit pacing and lit another cigarette.

"What the hell does that mean?" I asked.

"Mat, he . . . uh . . ." He went silent again.

"What did Mat do?" I asked. I moved closer to him.

"I might as well tell you. He dropped off a backpack, when I was gone. It had poems he'd written, a few other things—his stuff, man. He left a note with the pack. It only said, 'See you later,' and he signed it with a capital *M*, like he does. I assumed he was running away again, and he wanted me to keep his stuff. I'm still holding it for him."

"You tell that to George, or Rob López?"

"No. I mean, Mat and his father have a strained relationship, to put it mildly. I understood that if he left anything with me, it wasn't for George to know. I didn't want to be in the middle of that. I'm not a popular guy around here as it is, but, unfortunately, that's the kind of dynamic going on in that house. And if I couldn't tell George, then I had to keep quiet about it to the cop, too."

"But now you tell me? Someone you just met?"

"Tell you the truth, I'm worried. Mat's been gone a long time and he hasn't tried to contact me. I'm afraid something's happened. I was going to take the backpack to López. I feel like I've gotta do something. It's been too long." He sucked in a long draw of smoke, held it for a few seconds, then let it out through his mouth and nostrils. "You represent the family, right? I assume you'll tell George since you're working for him. But I'll take it to López. I think I have to."

"Yeah, all that sounds right. Where's the pack?"

He tossed his cigarette and motioned for me to follow him into the trailer.

The interior looked a lot like the outside. Trashed, dirty, dark and used up. Delgado disappeared into the back of the trailer. I heard him moving boxes and papers, and he dropped something that clanged like metal.

"Goddamn!" he shouted.

He stood in the shadows and shook his head.

"Can you fucking believe it? It's gone. Someone's taken it. Why would anyone do that?" He continued to shake his head while he spasmodically waved his fingers, as though he could pluck an answer to his questions from the stale trailer air. "There wasn't anything valuable in it. Just stuff that a teenaged boy would keep. Nothing, really. Why?"

"More important," I said. "Who?"

Four

On the way back to town, I tried to pry more information out of Delgado. He slumped in my pickup's seat with a pained look on his face, as though the idea that someone would sneak into his trailer and steal something was the absolute worst. Somebody had betrayed him, and I thought he knew who it was. But he wouldn't give me a name. I asked who knew about the backpack, who had access to his trailer and who would have a reason for snatching the pack. Nada, nothing. He mumbled that he couldn't believe it, and more than once he said that I should turn around and take him back to his place. I ignored him, and he avoided answering my questions.

I dropped the idea of learning more about the missing backpack and changed the subject.

"When Mat ran off before, did he have a favorite place to go, or maybe somebody he always met up with?"

"No, he never mentioned anyone specific to me."

"A place? Any clue where he headed from here?"

"I told you, I don't know anything else about Mat. All I had relating to Mat was that backpack. And now I don't even have that."

"He never talked about the places he visited, or what he did when he got somewhere?"

"No, he didn't. Mat isn't a talkative type of kid. Quiet and low key. That's Mat."

Maybe he just didn't talk to you, I thought. I wasn't going to let him off the hook. "I've been told he went to Pueblo, New Mexico, Denver. Anywhere else?"

"Jesus, man. What can I say? Yeah, he made it to those places. And he said once that he had a real good time in Pueblo. Big deal.

How hard is it to have a good time anywhere? He never explained what he meant by that. And I didn't ask."

He didn't say anything for the rest of our trip.

I parked at the police headquarters that also served as the city jail. The small building was far from impressive with its dark, peeling wood and dust-caked windows.

Delgado followed me into the building and then hesitated at the door of an enclosed office on the first floor. A solid-looking man in a brown uniform sat at an old wooden desk in the middle of the office.

I told the cop who I was and shook his hand. He frowned at Delgado.

"I'm Rob López," the cop said.

I gave him a short outline of what Delgado had told me about the missing backpack and the possible break-in at his trailer. Delgado nodded in agreement.

"You're under arrest, Wes." López grabbed Delgado by the elbow.

"What? You gotta be joking. What the fuck is going on?"

"You lied to me, Wes. When I talked to you about the missing boy, you denied you knew anything about him leaving. Now I learn that, in fact, you knew he was leaving and you had something of Mat's that could help in finding him. That's at least obstruction, not to mention providing false information, *and* interference. Let's go, you know the way to the cell."

López rushed him to the back of the building.

I wasn't sure about the legal basis for the lockup, but that didn't faze López or Delgado. Maybe lying was enough. It would've been in Denver. López was a cop, after all. And everyone knows you shouldn't lie to the cops.

I'd checked on López before I left Denver. I knew he had a badge and a gun, and a Jeep Wrangler with a siren. He also had a thin, not quite invisible birthmark that cut across his forehead, as though someone had botched a scalping. And he had a sturdy, almost chubby frame. He was the head man of a department that included him and two volunteers who together amounted to a half-time cop. He reminded me of guys I'd met in prison. Not guards, but inmates. His eyes never stopped surveying the scene, but they also never looked me in the face. He tapped the holster and gun on his hip when he wasn't tapping his booted feet. He seemed to be always moving, back and forth or in small circles. He increased my anxiety level just by talking. He was defensive, secretive and wary—traits found in any good cop. I guessed he enjoyed intimidating anyone who tried to get away with whatever passed for criminal activity in quiet, worn-out, almost deserted Melton, Colorado.

"George told me his cousin was going to dig around for Mat," López said when he returned from escorting Delgado to his cell.

He didn't sound like my presence bothered him. Just one of the facts.

"We looked, you know. He's not here, guarantee that. I told George to consider him gone, and one day he'll show up. Kids do that all the time. There's nothing in Melton to hold them, but once they get a taste of life in the so-called real world, they come running back to momma, usually in worse shape than when they left."

"You think Mat's okay? Just not telling anybody where he is?"

"Basically, yeah. And maybe he won't ever come back. That's happened, too. Life out here is hard and dull with occasional periods of boredom and maybe a tornado or two. I don't blame kids for running off."

"What kind of kid was Mat? I've heard what his family and his best friend think of him. How about you?"

He eased his body onto a too-small wooden chair behind his desk and twisted the cap on a plastic bottle of water. He lifted the water in my direction. I shook my head and he chugged from the bottle.

"Mat and his friends are like any kid," he said when he finished his drink. "They look for things to do. Anything. Sometimes they get carried away. Lightweight stuff, mostly. Joy rides on the bluffs, skinny dipping in the creek when it's got water, fights over girls. Boys his age drink beer, smoke marijuana, get girls pregnant. It's been that way for as long as I can remember. Mat did his share of carousing, but nothing unusual."

López had transferred his jumpy energy from walking in circles to talking about the missing boy. I listened and responded when he paused.

"No pregnant girlfriends?" I asked.

He chuckled. "Nah. Guess he was careful." He grinned and shook his head. "He had his share of girlfriends. Oh yeah. Real lover boy. A father or two might've had a thing against Mat, but he could charm anybody, including old school ranchers and farmers. Mat was smart, but you probably know that. Smart and ambitious. A handful for George. Mat and George have a hard time living in the same house. Again, I assume you know that. It's no surprise those two fought and argued. But like I say, nothing unusual. Every boy in the high school's senior class has had a blowout of some kind or another with their father. Just the way it is, and Mat and George are included in that."

"No reason to think that Mat's in trouble, or hurt, or worse?"

His eyes quit moving and he finally looked directly at me.

"If I thought he was in danger, I'd be looking for him night and day, with help from the sheriff. I've reported him missing to the CBI and sent notices to every damn police and sheriff's department in this part of the state. I beat the bushes for him. I even talked with my former boss in the Pueblo Police Department. He said he would do what he could and let me know if anything or anyone turned up that had a connection to the boy. I do my job, Corral."

"I'm not saying otherwise. Just want to know what you're thinking, that's all. I get it, you don't think Mat's in trouble."

"Oh, hell," he said "he might be in trouble. I didn't say otherwise. He's a teenage boy on his own. Could be all kinds of trouble. But I don't think he's in danger, and I also believe that he's missing because he wants to be, not because of something or someone else.

I know you're considering all possibilities. That's your job, I guess. And you've already given me something I didn't have before: Delgado's story about the backpack. More power to you. If you dig up something, I'll be on it. Like I'm gonna follow up with Delgado and the mysterious backpack." His tone told me he thought he'd be wasting time, but he'd do it.

"What about that stolen backpack?" I asked. "Who would do that?"

He chuckled again, louder this time. "That goddamn Delgado. He probably lost the pack, or he never had it. The man is a druggie and a clown. He had me fooled for a while, but he can't hide the fact that he's a loser, a mooch. If anything, he got high one night on LSD or another psychedelic, and he buried the backpack in the scrub grass as an offering to one of his spirit animals. Or whatever he's worshipping this month. He's a tripper, nothing more."

"Yet, you arrested him."

"Hell yes. He admitted he withheld evidence in a case of a missing boy. It may all be in his head, but until I know better, he stays in his cell. Maybe he'll dry out and remember what the hell he did with the backpack. Or that he never had such a thing."

He tried to minimize everything about Mat's disappearance. It might've been to protect his professional standing in the town. After all, it had taken me only a few hours to uncover evidence that he'd never heard about, and for me to learn that one of Mat's friends knew more about his leaving than anyone suspected. He absolutely did not want to consider that something bad had happened to Mat. I had to respect his instincts and his history in Melton. I'd go with them, and him, up to a point. I had to be cautious about jumping to conclusions if I wanted to do right by George and Essie.

Maybe López was right. Mat could've been a runaway who escaped to a different world, and it was as simple as that. But in the back of my foggy head, I had to wonder why he wasn't more concerned about the boy or Delgado's story.

We talked for a few more minutes about how useless Delgado was until the cop reminded me that at the end of summer, night came on suddenly and forcefully, and I wouldn't have the luxury of streetlights or other traffic to guide me to Essie's house.

"Yeah, I better go," I said. "My truck's headlights aren't all that bright."

"Nothing to hold back the night around here. And you'll be alone." He stretched his hand for a goodbye handshake.

"I'm sure I'll be okay," I said as I shook his hand.

"You want me to lead the way?" It wasn't a sincere offer.

"No, thanks. Really, I'll be okay."

"If you say so. Your funeral." He escorted me to the main door and patted my back. "If you have any more questions, I can usually be found here."

I pushed the heavy door and stepped into the street. The fading daylight washed over me. I heard López say, "Gotta give George his money's worth, right?"

I sat in my truck for several minutes and thought over what he'd said, and what Delgado had told me. While I tried to piece it together, López rushed from his poor excuse of a police headquarters and looked surprised when he saw my truck still parked in the street. He offhandedly waved and drove off. I started my pickup and turned it in the direction of the orange sunset that shimmered over the far black edge of Eastern Colorado.

Five

I felt like I was sucked into a black bag as soon as I left the town limits and turned onto Deer Lick Way, the road to Essie's house. I concentrated on the stretch of road lit by my headlights, and I told myself that I was driving in the quiet and peaceful countryside, nothing to worry about. No rush hour madness, no out-of-control truckers, no drunk office workers speeding to the next happy hour. I breathed in, deep and full. There had been a time when I would have believed those thoughts and the ride wouldn't have meant anything to me except a way to get to where I would sleep, but that was before my dented head and warped imagination. Now, I turned to the darkest alternative.

I followed Essie's directions, and for a few miles my phone's GPS worked. But when I climbed a small hill and then sunk below the horizon, my phone went blank and Essie's words jumbled together in my memory.

"It's not that hard," I whispered in the narrow cab of my pickup. "Focus, man."

The truck's smell of grease and sweat reassured me. The smooth-running Chevy six-banger gave me confidence. I relaxed and remembered that Essie said to watch for a sign with an arrow pointing to Gilroy Road.

I picked up speed on the downslope of the hill. The sky was dotted with stars never seen in the city. Night draped over my faded pickup. I cruised, faster than I should have. Images of Wes Delgado and Rob López mixed with the photographs of Mat that George had given me. I worried about Mat and couldn't avoid the darkest thoughts about what had happened to him.

I almost drove past the sign that appeared suddenly in my headlights. I slammed the brakes and the pickup fishtailed on the gravel road. I wrenched the oversized steering wheel and hoped I'd stay on the gravel. I didn't. The truck swayed and rocked, and I ended up turned around in the shoulder's soft dirt. The sudden stop killed my engine.

My headlights flickered and I turned them off. I could see only blackness. I started to sweat. I felt dizzy, and a hot flash confirmed I was in panic mode, although nothing serious had happened. I took in deeper breaths of air. I pumped the gas pedal and turned the key. I did that too many times and stopped only when I accepted that I'd flooded the engine. "You dumb fucker," I said to myself.

I had to wait to try to start the truck again. I leaned back against my ex's old blanket.

Again, my thinking turned to Delgado and López. I didn't like either one, but that wasn't anything new for me. I'd always been a skeptical guy, a Northside kid who didn't trust anyone who wasn't his sister. It was a given that I wouldn't feel comfortable around the police chief, and Wes Delgado . . . well he was just too weird.

I needed to make another run at him, loosen up all that he knew about where Mat Montoya might have gone and why he had left. I began to make a list of questions for Delgado.

The motion to my right was small, nothing more than a smoky wisp rustling the sage. But then it happened again.

I turned on the headlights. Off to the side, someone ducked to the ground. Someone with long hair.

I jumped from the cab and landed on soft earth that gave way under my weight, causing me to roll on the ground, almost brushing up against a cactus.

"Jesus!" I shouted.

I struggled to my feet and ran to where I'd seen the longhaired person. At least, I thought I'd seen someone. I stumbled again on rocks and loose dirt, fell to my knees and cursed. I waited and listened. Nothing. I stayed on my knees. My eyes adjusted to the darkness and strange unearthly objects slowly morphed into boulders, bushes and sandy mounds.

The only movement came from the slight breeze that caressed the scrub bushes. The night turned a deep purple, the stars overhead exploded and soared as though the sky moved, dragging me along, forcing me to stand up and then to holler with all the energy my depleted soul could muster.

"Mat! Mat Montoya! I'm your uncle, Gus. Your family needs to see you. Mat! Talk to me. Let me take you home."

The moon answered with silence. The stars ignored me. Whoever or whatever I'd seen was gone.

≫ ≫ ≫

"It wasn't Mat. Couldn't be." Essie didn't believe that I'd seen her missing nephew. She didn't believe much of my story, including the missing backpack left with Delgado. She had no problem with the idea that Delgado had been arrested.

I found her house fifteen minutes after my truck started. All I had to do was remember Essie's directions. She waited for me with a meal of beans, corn, green chile, fried pork chops and tortillas. Felisa, her mother, sat in a stuffed chair and stared at a television set. A lacy black shawl covered her arms. If my "aunt" recognized me, she didn't let on. Essie explained that she'd fed her mother earlier and that we shouldn't disturb her while she watched *Family Feud*.

I ate until my gut ached. It had been a long day and night.

"If it was Mat, why wouldn't he answer you?" she said. "Or come home, or here, to my house? He knows he can stay here whenever he wants. There's no need for him to be running around like a wild animal. No need at all."

I nodded but didn't interrupt her.

"And I never saw Mat write any poetry," she insisted. "Delgado's lying, for some reason, I don't know why. He's lying about the backpack, which I never saw with Mat. That's just Delgado bullshit. Even when he thought he was in love, Mat didn't write poems. He's not that kind of boy. Not a poet. He would've told me. He told me everything. He would've shown me any poems he'd written. That I do know."

"What do you mean, he was in love? With whom? When?"

She picked up my plate and fork and turned on the sink's faucet. I jumped to my feet and insisted that she let me do the dishes. She shrugged, then sat back down at her kitchen table. While I washed and rinsed, she told me about Mat and Yvonne Cleary, the dark-haired heartbreaker who'd left Mat in shambles.

"But that was almost a year ago."

"How serious was it?"

She nibbled on her lower lip before she answered. "Yvonne is a popular girl. She'd been dating Connor, and a few others. Then Mat, then back to Connor. I told him to be careful with her, but he's a hard-headed teenager as set in his ways as his father. Anyway, eventually, he moved on from her, dated other girls from his class. He took the breakup hard, but he bounced back. I know he was hurting for a long time, but then he wised up. That's his words. He told me, months ago, at his father's birthday party, that he couldn't believe what he'd put up with from Yvonne. He was so over her. That was obvious."

"She'd been dating Connor?"

"Yeah, but they weren't that serious. Not from what I could see. They were off and on. Connor seemed relieved when they finally ended it. Connor and Mat were okay, still friends, if that's what you're getting at."

"I'm trying to see the whole picture."

"Sure, whatever." Her eyes stayed on me.

"What?" I said. "What's on your mind?"

"Oh, nothing really. I, uh, I'm worried about you. You sure you're okay? You doing all right?"

"You mean because of my headaches, and all? Maybe I'm not up to the job? Maybe I'm seeing things, like the vanishing ghost out in the night?"

"I didn't mean it that way, Gus. I am worried, of course. About Mat, mostly, but you, too. I don't want you to get hurt, or anything like that."

"Why would I get hurt? Where's that coming from?"

She grabbed my hand and squeezed it. "I'm sorry. I'm screwing this up. I want you to know I'm here if you need help. That's all. Nothing more. I guess Mat's disappearance has me more upset than I thought. I'm sorry."

"If there's any time when you think I'm messing up, all you have to do is tell me. I'll believe it. I get that from Corrine. I'm used to it. But for now, I'm good, and I'm going to do the job you and George want. If I can't deliver, I'll take off and quit bothering you."

She clenched her jaw and nodded. I continued to do the dishes.

"I should talk with her," I said while I wiped my coffee cup.

"Yvonne? Why?" Essie asked. "That relationship was a while back. I doubt Mat said more than a half-dozen words to her in the past six months. They weren't in contact. It wasn't like that."

Essie believed she knew all about Mat, but she had only a few pieces of his puzzle. If I was going to do my job right, I had to talk to as many people as possible, maybe everybody in town. There had to be much more to learn about Matías Montoya. And, somehow, I had to figure out whether that really had been Mat out in the country darkness. I'd seen somebody, or something. But I wasn't certain of anything else.

"She's part of Mat's world," I said. "No matter what happened between them. I'll need your help to talk with her. Maybe Alicia can do it if you don't want to. They friends?"

"No. Alicia and Yvonne have nothing in common. They move in different circles. Alicia's never liked Yvonne. Don't ask her." Her shoulders dropped an inch. "If you insist, I can take you to her, tomorrow."

"That'll work."

"I'll call her in the morning."

I put away the dried cups and plates and waited for Essie to talk again. I wasn't sure what I'd done, but something had upset her. *Gus Corral stepping on toes, as usual. Was that it?*

"Gus," she finally said. "The people out here. We're different. We mind our business and don't appreciate anyone mixing in our privacy, no matter the intention. That's a big reason why most of us are still living in Melton. We'll give our neighbor our last piece of bread, or the last dollar we got in our purse. And everyone gets paid back, usually with interest. But we need our space. We don't want even our neighbors to cross into that space unless we ask them to."

"That's obvious, Essie. Look where you live. Plenty of space around here, too much for me, you want to know the truth. And not many Mexicans."

"There's a few. We've been here a long time, but most people assume we're newcomers, immigrants."

"Yeah, I get it. Same thing happens in Denver. Anyway, I understand about your need for space. Even I get tired of the city. That's one reason I took on this job for George. I had to get away. If you're saying that Yvonne or her family are gonna resent me or not want to talk with me, I can deal with that. I get the same thing in Denver. But if you want me to do my best to find out what happened to Mat, these are the kinds of things I have to do, including interrupting someone's sense of privacy."

She nodded. "I know. I know. I'm worried and I wish that you could just tell us where Mat is, and we could move on. I guess it's gonna take some time."

"We'll get answers, I promise that."

She smiled. I regretted that I might have given her false hope. But that's why I was in Melton, wasn't it? That was me, Mr. Hopeful. Just don't call me Mr. Pitiful.

"What about Mat's teachers?" I asked. "Is there one he was closer to than the others? Can you think of someone else I should talk to? Another friend, a coach, maybe a relative I don't remember?"

She thought for a few seconds then nodded her head.

"Susan O'Brien. Mat told me he liked her classes. She teaches math and science at the high school, and she coached the girls' volleyball team and worked out routines for the cheerleaders. Yvonne was on the team last year. And a cheerleader. Mat told me that he got to know O'Brien through Yvonne. Susan was his Biology teacher, but he didn't really know her until he started hanging out with Yvonne. After Mat and Yvonne broke up, he didn't talk about the teacher anymore. She doesn't know anything more than what you already know. I met with her, two weeks ago, but she didn't add anything. I think you'd get more from the school principal, Gloria Ahern, but she's on vacation. If you want to talk to someone else, Susan's probably your next interview. Her and Yvonne."

She led me from the kitchen to the front room. Her mother had fallen asleep in the armchair that surrounded her like a chubby baby elephant. The wrinkled yellowish woman snored slightly. Broken front teeth and the tip of a pale tongue peeked through a smile the old woman wore while she slept.

I sat down and stared at the end of the game show Felisa had been watching. Essie disappeared for a few minutes, then returned with a blanket. She covered her mother and turned down the television's volume.

A pair of candles flickered on a side table near the TV.

"Are those for Mat?" I asked.

Essie nodded. "One is mine, the other's my mother's. She insisted we light them when we realized Mat wasn't coming home like the other times. She's vowed to keep them lit until he returns."

"Corrine did the same thing. She lit a candle when I left Denver. She said it was for Mat, but it's probably as much for me. She worries about me. Too much."

"That's what sisters are for. Be thankful you have two."

"You bet." I don't think she saw me roll my eyes.

"You can sleep in the extra room," she said. "Clean sheets, and close to the bathroom. My mother will sleep here for another hour or so, then she'll wake up and I'll move her to her own room. I've got to do some work, but I'll be in my room if you need anything."

"I'm gonna call it a night."

"Okay. In the morning, we'll have breakfast, then we can go find *las güeras*, the two white women, Yvonne and Susan. Come on, I'll show you your room."

I nodded and followed my cousin through her spacious house. She pointed to the bathroom and said, "Shower's in there," then handed me a towel and an extra blanket. We ended up at a back room with a big bed and paintings of rundown wooden buildings.

"Where'd these come from?" I asked. I nodded at one of the framed shacks.

"I painted them, years ago. It was a phase."

"They're good. I can see the scars and marks in the old wood. Very nice."

"Thanks. They're buildings that've been around here for more than a hundred years. At least, they used to be. Some of them have fallen apart since I painted them. I don't do that anymore."

She left, and I heard the door to her room close. I brushed my teeth and then fell asleep without reviewing the day's events. All I really knew was that I was tired, and I'd only begun my job.

Six

Rain pelted Essie's house around midnight for twenty minutes. Lightning lit up the room. My legs jerked at the sounds of breaking thunder and rainwater rushing through the house's gutters. The fertile smell of the soaked earth floated on the heavy air. My last thought before I fell asleep was about Mat, or whoever it was, and whether he'd found shelter from the storm.

I woke up around five, normal for me. I stayed in bed and watched the sun break through the curtains and then slowly, one-by-one, spotlight Essie's paintings. I'd slept off and on, sometimes dreaming about the wispy figure I saw in the scrub, other times of finding Mat's body. The wet earth smell lingered.

When I finally did wake completely, the silence pressed on me like an old musty quilt. No sounds in the house, nothing outside. Essie's house was far enough away from the town that traffic noise couldn't penetrate the quiet. But, of course, Melton didn't suffer the chaos of a rush hour.

I had a vague bad feeling—again, normal for me. The missing teenager had been gone too long. If he wasn't hurt, or dead, then he was too far away or so deep on the run that I would never find him. For a few minutes I convinced myself that I should tell George that my work was over and he would have to wait for something from Mat or the police. But as the room warmed up and more light filtered around me, I knew I couldn't do that to George or Essie. I hadn't earned the right to kill their hope. Not yet. And Corrine would never let me live down the fact that I'd cracked out on my first investigative job for someone in the family. No, I'd stick it out until the mystery of Mat Montoya was solved, one way or another.

I was halfway down the hall to the shower when a door opened and Felisa poked her head out of the doorway. She smiled and nodded at me. She leaned against a walker and hummed a lively tune I didn't recognize.

"Good morning, Mrs. Montoya," I said.

"*Buenos días*, Mr. Corral. Nice rain, last night, no?" She didn't give me a chance to answer. "You're Alejandra's boy, ain't you? Your father was Esteban Corral? You remember me? I knew your parents, way back when. Good people. *¿Cómo no? Sí, verdad.* We had some good times, don't you know?"

"Of course," I said. "My mother used to tell me stories about the family reunions, the Christmas parties."

"Long time ago. But I remember like it was yesterday." She closed her eyes.

I moved a step closer to the bathroom.

"You're looking for Matías, no?" she asked without opening her eyes. "That boy . . . he's a good boy, I love him, don't you know?" She opened her eyes and shook her head. Long gray strands of hair caressed her neck and shoulders. "But he has too much going on in that brain of his, you know. Gets him all mixed up sometimes. Good boy, but he does what he wants, not always thinking. Boys, eh?" She stepped back into her room. "When you find him, tell him that his grandma wants to talk to him. I got some things to tell him. He'll know what you mean."

She shut the door, and I heard the walker scrape across the floor. She must have turned on a radio. The classic Mexican song *Un puño de tierra* followed me.

※ ※ ※

Before Essie and I left the house, George called, and I filled him in on what had happened with Delgado and López and my misadventure on the way to Essie's house. I assumed he'd have the same concerns about me as Essie, but he laughed when I told him Delgado had been arrested and laughed harder when I mentioned seeing something in the darkness.

"Oh, hell," he said, "that's just the ghost of Running Elk, the old Indian chief that was killed around here back in the pioneer days. He cursed all white men before he died, and he prowls the prairie looking for scalps. But you're not white, so you should be okay. I'm surprised Essie didn't clear that up for you."

"You're not serious, right?"

Another laugh. "No, of course not. It's a silly story people tell their kids to make them behave. What you saw and heard, or thought you heard, was probably an animal, a prairie dog or maybe an injured antelope separated from its herd. This is the country out here, you know. But you got to be careful if you're wandering around. These grasslands are home to snakes and coyotes and even wild dogs. A mountain lion now and then, a bear occasionally, like every ten years."

"What I saw looked more human than like any bear or coyote."

"You sure about what you saw?"

There it was. A hint of doubt in George's voice. A hesitation that meant he was thinking over what he knew about me and how much trust he could put into what I told him. Maybe I was the crazy cousin from the city, and not much else.

"Can't be sure of anything, George," I said. "Not about what I saw or heard out there, at night, especially when it was gone before I could do anything. It only lasted a few seconds."

"I should've gone with you. Next time you're gonna be out at night, I'm with you. I'll be your guide or whatever. I need to do something, anyway. Need to help. Mat needs my help."

"Sure, makes sense." I was trying to reassure myself as much as George.

George said he had to get to work and he reminded me to call on him for help.

"I'll drop by your shop later," I said. "We can go over everything then."

"Yeah, that's good. I'll be there all day."

Before he said goodbye, he asked to speak with Essie. They spoke for a minute or two, although Essie said only a few words. She nodded her head, several times, looked at me and hung up. Felisa smiled at us as we left the house.

"She'll be okay?" I asked.

"Alicia will be here in a few minutes. She spends time with her grandmother every day, or she tries to. When I have to leave the house, Alicia's a real help. It's more of a problem when she's in school. I don't like to leave my mother alone."

I drove into town and filled up the gas tank before we made our way to Melton's lone coffee shop, Pinki's Pies and Pour-Purree.

Essie had called Susan O'Brien the night before, when she took a break from working in her room, and the two agreed to meet at the coffee shop. O'Brien wore blue shorts and a yellow cowboy shirt with pearl-like buttons. She greeted Essie with a big smile and the two hugged like old friends. She shook my hand when Essie introduced me as her private-eye cousin. Essie and I ordered coffee, then we sat at O'Brien's table.

"Still nothing from Mat?" the teacher asked.

"No, nothing," Essie said. "I'm so worried, I can't think right. Gus is doing what he can, and he thought that he should talk with you. Like I explained last night on the phone, he doesn't want to miss anything."

"Sure, sure," O'Brien said. "I understand, and I'll do what I can to help, but I'm afraid there isn't much I can offer. Not more than I've told you, Essie. Nothing's changed."

"And I get that, too," I said. "But one never knows. I mean, I don't want to be a pest . . ."

"Oh, no. It's okay," O'Brien said. "I'll do anything to help."

"It'll be good for me to hear what you know about Mat and his latest disappearance. Start anywhere. Whatever pops in your head."

She clasped her hands together and shrugged her shoulders. The woman behind the counter motioned at Essie that our drinks were ready. A few minutes passed before we got back to talking about Mat.

Bright yellow hair framed O'Brien's round face. Her skin was tanned by the sun, just like everyone else I'd met from Melton. She pursed her thin lips before she spoke.

"Mat is a special kid," she said. "Teachers say that about their students all the time, but with Mat it's something else. He's smart, we all know that. He reads everything he can get his hands on; he spends time in libraries and bookstores. That's what he does when he runs off to other cities and towns. Well, one of the things he does. He knows what's happening in the world, and he has solid opinions about politics, religion, you name it. He's not your average seventeen-year-old."

"That's Mat, no doubt," Essie said. "Always reading, or arguing, especially with his father. Well, not arguing—wrong word. I shouldn't have said that. More like *debating.* George and Mat like to challenge each other."

O'Brien nodded. "Yeah, he's good at holding his own when it comes to opinions and what he thinks should be done about whatever world crisis he's focusing on. He told me he wanted to go to college some place completely different from Melton. I said he'd get homesick, but he laughed that off, and I think he was right. Melton is too small for Mat."

"That's why he runs away?" I asked. "He needs to see the world. That it?"

O'Brien looked away to the empty street. "I don't want to cause trouble, but . . ."

"But, what?"

"Mat often talked about how he couldn't keep on with his father, George. I'm sorry, Essie. I don't mean in any really bad way, just that they were too much alike. That's what Mat said. Too similar to get along. He needed to get away, he told me. I think Mat grew up too fast, after his mother died. And he needed more room than George gives him."

"It's not that bad, Susan," Essie said.

"I don't mean it the way it sounds. It's coming out all wrong. George is a wonderful father. After Cindy died, he did a great job raising Mat and Alicia on his own. And Mat says that, too. He's proud of his father. His military service, the way he's made a name and a place for himself here. It's not that Mat hates his father, he just, oh . . . I don't know, he just needs more room than George can give him," like I said.

Tears leaked from her eyes, and I remembered that Connor and Alicia had teared up when they talked about Mat.

"Where did Mat go when he left in the past?" I asked. I could already see myself driving to pick up Mat's trail.

"Pueblo, Colorado Springs, Denver. Once he made it as far as Albuquerque before he called George to go pick him up."

"Any special place in those towns?"

She stared through the shop's window at a dog running across the street. "He mentioned a place in Pueblo where he slept a few nights. A shelter for kids. He said he had important work in Pueblo. That's what he called it. 'Meaningful,' he said. He didn't elaborate but he must've been talking about the shelter. I think he said it was called the Sunrise, or Rising Sun, something like that."

"That's good. I'll dig into that. And this time? You know where he was planning to go?"

Albuquerque would be a long slow ride in my truck.

She drank some coffee and cleared her throat. "No, no. I didn't know he was leaving. The last time we talked, a couple of days before he was gone, he told me that he and Connor were talking about hitting the road, that's what he called it, but he also said he'd let everyone know when they were leaving. He didn't want anyone to worry about him. But then he left without Connor and he didn't tell anyone. At least, he didn't talk to me."

"Connor said that he and Mat were talking about going to Denver, but only for a weekend," I said. "That what Mat meant?"

Susan shook her head. "I got the impression it was more than simply a weekend in the city. He said Connor was as ready as he was, they only needed time to get ready. The trip wasn't happening for a while, though, and I thought Mat would be with Connor. In my mind, that meant that they'd be back before long. Connor's not the type to run away. He's not that kid."

"What kind of kid is he?" I asked.

"That's a strange question."

"I'm only trying to get background. If I understand Mat's friends, I might better understand Mat. Maybe it'll help me figure out what he's up to. That's all I meant."

"Connor's Mat's best friend," the teacher said. "They've been friends since the first grade. Connor and Mat are more like brothers than simply friends."

"You're saying Connor wouldn't run away with Mat, but he would take off with him for . . . what? A long weekend? A little more?"

O'Brien looked like she could break down any minute. The strain of not knowing what happened to her favorite pupil had etched worry lines and shadows around her eyes. At least, that's what I assumed. She'd reluctantly answered my question about Connor, but I didn't think that meant too much. She came off as a teacher protecting her students. And I was the unknown outsider.

Compared to the teacher, Essie was much calmer, more at ease, but that could've been a cover to hide her concern from the rest of her family, maybe an attempt to not stress out her mother or her niece Alicia. Every so often a note of anxiety crept into her voice.

"We should go, Essie."

She agreed, and we thanked Susan for her time and help. We left the teacher in the coffee shop, still on the verge of tears.

Next on my agenda was a conversation with Yvonne Cleary, Mat's former girlfriend. Essie had arranged a meeting with her at the assisted living residence where the girl volunteered.

Again, Essie warned me that the girl wouldn't know anything that could help.

I nodded. "What's her background?" I asked.

"Yvonne's father is the town doctor, the county's doctor, actually," Essie said as I drove down Melton's Main Street. "Robert Cleary. He's a local, older than you'd expect since he has a teenage daughter. The mother's Annie, from back East. She's younger than Robert, they met in college. I think he was a graduate student, maybe already in med school, and she was an undergrad. She comes from money. Old oil money. At least that's the impression she gives. Not sure any of that means *anything*."

"And how about Yvonne? What do you think of her?"

"Tell you the truth, I don't really like her. She's polite enough, and smart enough, and popular with other students. But Mat told me that there's not much beyond the obvious. Whenever I've interacted with her, it's like she can barely spare the time, know what I mean?"

"Mat dumped her, or the other way around?"

She paused. "She told Mat it was over after he took her to the homecoming dance. Caught him by surprise, and he was a basket case for a while."

"Why'd she break it off?"

"Mat wasn't specific about that. He said that she told him that she knew they would be going different ways when they graduated, and she didn't want to go through what all that meant, so she wanted to end it. I knew there was more to it, that she had another reason, but that was her excuse. I guess before it got too serious."

"But it was already serious for Mat."

"Yeah, poor kid. He was blindsided by her."

"Maybe that's why you don't like her."

She shrugged. "Could be."

"Well, we'll see if Yvonne can add anything. But I already know some of what I must do if I want to get on Mat's trail. I'll talk to Delgado again. He knows more than he told me, and there's something about that backpack story that's nagging at me, especially that someone would steal it. None of that makes sense. Not yet anyway. But after I finish with Delgado, I've got to go where Mat might have gone."

"You mean Pueblo, Colorado Springs?"

"Yeah. And Denver, too, maybe Albuquerque. And wherever else Mat has run off to in the past. I'll learn where Mat would go when he made it to those cities, then go there myself. Unless you have some other idea?" I asked.

"No, that sounds right." She jiggled her keys before she completed her thought. "But you should go over that with George, don't you think?"

"Yeah, you're right. I'm visiting George later. I can tell him what I'm thinking."

"Maybe he'll want to go with you. You should ask him. He needs to be more involved."

"Be okay with me. Probably for the best."

I didn't want anyone to tag along with me, but I couldn't say that to Essie. If George wanted to ride with me when I looked for his son, there was no way I could tell him no.

Essie's phone buzzed. She listened, nodded her head a couple of times and finally said, "Yes, sure. We'll be there. We're on our way now."

I waited for her to explain.

"They want us at their house, not the seniors' residence." Essie talked as she put away her phone. "We're meeting with the whole family."

※ ※ ※

Yvonne Cleary and her parents waited for us in a large house on the eastern edge of town, the opposite side of Melton from where Essie and George lived. The two-story structure, plus an attic surrounded by a balcony, a separate greenhouse and an attached two-car garage, reflected white sunlight off its gleaming white paint with blue trim. A neat lawn flanked a driveway where a new hybrid Toyota sat in the shade of an elm tree. Late summer flowers and well-trimmed bushes ringed the foundation of the house. Bamboo sunshades gently swayed in the breeze that drifted through the covered porch. Everything about the house said status and success.

The reception from the Cleary family was cold, to say the least. Yvonne sat in an upholstered straight-back chair and hardly looked at Essie or me as we sat on an antique-looking couch that had all the comfort of a cement bench. The father, the good doctor, raised his eyebrows when Essie explained that I was an investigator from Denver, and her cousin, and that I was looking for Mat. He slouched next to his wife, his back curved and floppy like an over-cooked piece of spaghetti.

The mother, meanwhile, couldn't stop staring at my faded jeans and greasy sneakers. Well, she couldn't stop staring at me. I might've reminded her of the farmworkers that spent a couple of weeks in the area every picking season when the few farmers around Melton needed help with the alfalfa or wheat harvests. I knew what she was thinking. I was as dark as any field hand, as scruffy as any vagrant and stranger than anything the rich woman from the East Coast had ever allowed in her impressive house. She stood behind Yvonne with her hands on the girl's shoulders, ready to fling herself at me if I made a provocative move towards her daughter. Or so I believed. Not just believed, though. I was convinced, dead certain. I hoped I wouldn't regret asking for the meeting.

"I already told Essie and Mat's father everything I knew about Mat's plans," Yvonne said when I asked her about Mat's intention to leave town. Her voice was subdued but I detected an edge to it, a note of resentment, and maybe some fatigue.

"Yes, but it would help if you could tell me, again," I said. "I'm trying to help. You want to help, don't you?"

"I'm not sure I like your tone, Mr. Corral," the doctor said.

"Where's that coming from?" I said. He surprised me and I wanted to tell him that I could adopt a tone if I had to, and I was sure he wouldn't like it.

Cleary lifted his shoulders and straightened his spine. "My daughter has been completely cooperative with Mat's family and the police. Chief López spent more than an hour with her. If Yvonne says she's given all the information she has about Mat and his chronic running away, then that's it."

I forced myself to apologize. "I'm sorry about my tone, Doctor Cleary. I don't want to offend. But, honestly, I don't understand why there's any kind of problem. I'm sure we all want to find out what happened to Mat. If he's in any kind of trouble or danger you want to help, don't you?"

"Really, that's ridiculous," Mrs. Cleary said. Her voice was high, strained, but under control. "Mat's not in danger or trouble. He's run away, again. That's all there is to it."

"We are worried, Annie," Essie said. "George and I are trying to do all we can to find him. He's not just run away. This is different, he's been gone too long. And all we are asking is for Yvonne to tell us what she can. Nothing more."

Before Yvonne could respond, the mother stepped in front of her and spoke to Essie directly. "The boy has no sense of responsibility, no idea what it means to be a grown-up. Yvonne's contact with him was not anything serious, and it didn't last long."

She stopped talking so suddenly that I wouldn't have been surprised if she'd lost her voice. I assumed she was reconsidering her words, that maybe she realized she was out-of-line. Instead, somewhere deep inside Mrs. Cleary, a dam broke. Her voice returned, an octave higher than before, faster, urgent, brittle.

"I think you have to leave," she said. "We don't want any of this, we don't want to be involved. The boy will turn up, as he has in the past. His father needs to manage him better, that's all. That would solve all this trouble. George has to keep him in line. You people don't know how to manage your children."

Essie jerked backwards and was about to say something when the doctor said, "Please go, please go." His mouth twisted into a wrinkled sliver of pale flesh.

Then he got up, walked to the front door and slowly opened it. Essie looked at me and motioned that we should go. I looked down at Yvonne. Her mouth matched her father's grimace. She gripped the arms of her chair so hard that her fingers turned bone white.

"If you think of anything, Yvonne, call Essie," I said. "It might help, and it is important."

Essie and I walked out of the house. The door slammed behind us. The mother said something, but I couldn't make out the words. Her voice was harsh and sharp. We heard Yvonne crying.

Seven

I steered my pickup back to Main Street. Essie sat on the edge of the blanketed truck seat, her hands clasped together in her lap. She hadn't said a word since we'd climbed into the cab, but I heard sighs and heavy breathing coming from her.

"That explains why Yvonne broke it off with Mat," I said.

"Those parents?" she blurted. "They blew me away. I didn't suspect they were like that, to that extreme. I just didn't want to believe it. I knew they had an attitude, that's not uncommon around here. I've seen it all my life. Mat said they weren't the people everyone thinks they are, but I didn't understand. I supposed he was only reacting to Yvonne throwing him over. I never would've guessed they were out-and-out racists."

"Something about me brought out the worst in them. I have that effect on people."

"It wasn't you, Gus. Annie . . . that bitch. I almost slapped her face. Can you believe that I've donated to her damn dog hospital fundraiser? She won't get any more of my money. And Yvonne. What a mess. She looked terrible. Sick, depressed. You'd think the doctor and his bitch wife would know better. Takes all kinds."

I tried to guide the conversation in a more productive direction. "It might be helpful if we could talk with Yvonne without her parents around. But that's for another day. Cleary will have me arrested if I try to approach his daughter again."

Essie sank back in her seat. "I'll talk with Alicia," she said. "Maybe she can think of a way, for me at least, to meet with Yvonne. Seriously, though, I don't think the girl knows anything else about Mat. It's clear as day now; her parents split them up as soon as they thought the relationship was getting serious, and then they must've kept Yvonne on a tight leash. No wonder Mat said he hadn't had any communication with her since they broke up."

The look on Annie Cleary's face triggered feelings I'd put away, years before. I remembered when I was ten years old and how angry my father became when my mother told him that a woman at the grocery store had called her a dirty Mexican because my mother had taken the last shopping cart. He demanded to know all the details—what did the woman say exactly, who heard her say it, what did my mother say—which my mother did not want to tell him. Then he wanted to know all he could about the woman—how old was she, what color was her car, what did she look like? My mother refused, even though she was crying and upset. "Leave it alone," she said to my father, more than a few times. It took an hour of him swearing and generally calling out all white people before he finally calmed down.

They never talked about the incident, but I never forgot it. I carried my father's anger and my mother's embarrassment until I realized, many mistakes later, that the weight was too much and I was the one who had to leave it alone. I had to let it go. And yet, on a beautiful late summer morning in the small town of Melton, Colorado, anger and embarrassment simmered in my guts and then settled at the bottom of my heart.

I parked in front of the police building. The street looked empty. Nothing new about that. Melton always looked empty, deserted. No window shoppers in front of the boarded-up stores, no cars lined up at the traffic lights. Dead town walking. A ghost town in the making.

No wonder Mat ran away, I thought.

Essie said she had to finish tax forms with one of her clients and that she would see me later at her house. She assured me that she would be okay. She jogged across the street, still uttering cuss words at Annie Cleary.

Chief López sat at his desk, in the same position as when I'd first found him in his office. He shuffled a pile of papers. A cigarette burned in an ashtray on his desk.

He stubbed it dead and said, "I'm quitting. Sometimes I light one and let it burn out. It's a hell of a habit."

"Whatever works," I answered.

"Sit down," he said. "Hope you have some info about Mat. I need good news. It's been a bad week."

He still looked like a sack of cats—jumpy, nervous.

"Can't say I have anything that you don't already know. I've only been on the job since yesterday."

"Seems longer, don't it? Melton can do that to a person. Heard about your run-in with the ghost of Running Elk. That must've been fun." His face lit up like a cheap flashlight about to burn out.

"How do you know about that? It barely happened last night."

He smiled. "In case you hadn't noticed, Melton's a very small town. Word travels fast around here. I don't know how it happens, but it's almost impossible to have a secret in this town. I know. I've tried. Sooner or later, everyone knows everyone else's business. That can make my job a lot easier or a lot more complicated. Depending on who and what."

I wondered how long it would take for the cop to hear all about my aborted meeting with the town doctor and his family. Essie had talked about the townspeople's reverence for the sacred sense of privacy. But the chief described a place where everyone knew everyone's business. The reality of life in a small town?

"People already know about you and what you're up to," he continued. "You're the talk of the town."

"You don't think I saw Mat Montoya?" I said. "I wasn't hallucinating. There was someone out there."

"Or something. No doubt. I believe you saw . . . an object, maybe a person, more likely an animal. Think about it. You were in the middle of a combo of grasses, weeds, cactus, wind, blowing dust. Together, especially at night, that stuff can look like anything."

"I only know what I saw."

"No doubt. I've had people sitting right where you are now, the Oakleys. They're good sober people, mature adults. They told me they ran over a space alien out there in the scrub. Said it scratched the paint on the utility trailer they were pulling. They claimed they even found a gooey oily liquid under the trailer. They said it had to be alien blood. I listened to them with a straight face and I did my duty, what they pay me for. Drove out there and looked around. When I checked out the scene of the alleged encounter, I found a broken piece of old dead cactus, nothing but cholla. I inspected the trailer, and yeah, its paint was scratched, but what trailer ain't got scratched paint, right? No gooey alien's blood. To this day, those people look for UFOs every night. They're afraid the aliens are gonna come for them and make them pay for running over one of the spacemen."

"What I saw wasn't a piece of cactus. It had long hair and it ducked away, not like an animal but like a man, or a boy."

"Okay, Gus. Tell you what. Let's go out there. We can go now, if you want. We'll search the area, look for signs of a human being who prowls in the dark around deserted dirt roads. What's he doing out there besides scaring the shit out of a Denver private dick? Why's he out there and not in his safe, comfy home, if in fact this person you saw is Mat Montoya? Far as I know, Mat was a regular teenager. Smart, yeah, and maybe more grown-up than the usual seventeen-year-old, but still a kid, nothing weird or out-of-kilter. So, why's he out there?"

"Look, I don't know if that was Mat. I saw something, it could've been Mat. I have no reason for why it would be him. You're probably right. I repeat: All I know is what I saw."

"You and Jerry and Bertha Oakley. You all know what you saw."

"I don't expect you to look for what I saw. In fact, the only reason I'm here is to talk with Delgado. I want to wrap up a few things with him. Then, I can move on. Get out of your hair."

"You done with your investigating? Back to Denver?"

"Not yet . . . I'll visit places Mat has run off to in the past. If that's what George wants. I'll talk with George when I'm finished with Delgado."

The cop looked disappointed. "George should save his money. Mat will turn up one of these days. But your cousin won't listen to me."

A loud crash from the direction of the jail cell interrupted our talk.

"What the . . . ?" López said as he jumped up and ran to the back.

I followed but I stayed out of his way.

Delgado hung by a sheet from the bars that blocked the cell's small window. He appeared to be unconscious, but his legs furiously kicked against the wall and his hands gripped the knotted sheet around his neck. The cot was tipped over and lay on its side.

"Goddamn! Goddamn!" López shouted as he rushed into the cell, gripped Delgado's legs and pushed up to relieve the pressure of the sheet on his neck.

"There's a knife in my desk," he hollered.

I ran to the desk, found the knife and ran it back to López. I grabbed Delgado's legs and López cut the knot. Together we lowered Delgado to the floor.

"I'll call Doc Cleary," López said. "We need him here."

"How about an ambulance? A hospital?"

"Too far away. Delgado needs attention now. Keep your eyes on this idiot."

He rushed to his desk and made the call.

I watched the delirious Delgado as he tossed and squirmed. He mumbled incoherently.

"Feeling guilty about something?" I said.

I was still waiting for an answer when Cleary showed up at the cell door with a medical bag and a surprised and worried look on his face.

≫≫ ≫≫ ≫≫

Cleary did what he could, and it looked like Delgado would live. The doctor's skill surprised me. He may not have relished the idea of treating someone like Delgado, but he was a professional the entire time, and he did appear concerned about the severity of his patient's injuries. I didn't say anything about our earlier meeting, and neither did he. In fact, he never acknowledged my presence. An ambulance finally arrived, and the EMTs rushed Delgado to the nearest hospital in Eads, a half-hour away. Cleary followed the ambulance in his own car. López and I cleaned up the cell and washed Delgado out of our hands and arms.

The cop said he needed a drink, so we walked over to the Sand Creek Saloon. Along the way, López talked about the strange character Delgado.

"He showed up one day and immediately got everyone worked up about a book he was writing and how it was gonna be about the people of Melton. He started talking to folks, hearing their stories, catching up on the history of the town. Yeah, he was a popular guy for a while."

"How long that last?"

"A month or two. It became obvious that he was all talk and no action. He must've been planning a con for a while. I figure his so-called interviews of people were just a way to get information, look at where folks live, maybe dig up a secret or two that he could use. He had a drug habit—painkillers, no surprise—and his addiction short-circuited his scam. Before you could say *get a job,* he owed money to just about everybody in town."

"He must be quite the con man if he convinced the straight-edged people of Melton to give him money."

"Oh yeah, he was good. He pocketed a nice chunk of change from investors in the book. Some of Melton's leading citizens couldn't resist the idea of having their name and family tree written up in a book that anyone could order online. With others, he simply borrowed and never paid them back. I have no proof, but

I'm convinced he was behind a string of break-ins, although he must've used a few of the village idiots to do the actual dirty work."

"He sounds like the wrong person for Mat to have for a friend."

"Yeah, although until you came in with Delgado yesterday, and he told that story about the backpack, I didn't think they were that close. If I'd known, I would've warned George."

"I'm surprised no one had him arrested."

"I have a file of complaints about him, but most of what happened wasn't really a crime, you know? Of course, Delgado will say he is still working on that damn book. I told the complainers that they had to sue Delgado. Take him to court to get back their money."

"Anyone do that?"

"Nah. Court sounds like nothing but a waste of time. And expensive. And since Delgado didn't have anything of value, why do it? People were fed up with Delgado, but after a while, they quit giving him money and they left him alone, for the most part."

"Somebody did something?"

"Sort of. Leroy Bannon, the rancher. You talked with him?"

"Right."

"Leroy confronted Delgado one day, last fall. Out there at Delgado's trailer. Bannon beat the crap out of him, for all the good that did him. I didn't blame Bannon. I thought about kicking Delgado's ass myself. Still, Bannon never got his money."

"You arrest Bannon?"

López smirked. "You really aren't from around here, are you? Don't work that way, not with one of the wealthiest and most influential ranchers in the county. Besides, Delgado wouldn't press charges. Wanted me to drop it, so I did. It worked out."

We got to the entrance of the bar and walked in.

"You might not like the way things played out for Delgado, or understand it, but this is a different way of life out here, Corral. You realize that, don't you?"

"I'm beginning to," I said. "I'm more interested on how any of this concerns Mat, and whether any of it will help me find him."

I followed the police chief up to the bar.

Nothing had changed about the Sand Creek Saloon, including the bar flies. The guy known as Werm bent over a glass of beer. He lifted his eyes when we sat on the other end of the bar, but he didn't otherwise move or make a sound. The jukebox still played country songs I didn't recognize. Freddy the bartender served up two bottles of beer and two shots of tequila, and López and I tried to drink away the image and smell of a man who'd decided he'd finally had enough.

"Why the hell did he do that?" I asked after we'd scorched our throats with the Cuervo.

"Why's anybody try to kill themselves?" López said. He signaled Freddy to pour two more shots. "Just couldn't deal with it anymore, whatever it is. Have to say, though, that I didn't expect that from Delgado. He's loopy and a con man, and good for nothin', but I'd never take him for a man who'd do himself in. Otherwise, I'd've transferred him to another town with a real jail, maybe Pueblo, and with twenty-four-hour guards. *Never* thought he'd try to hang himself."

"Tough way to go."

"Yeah, but he ain't gone. Which is too bad. Might've ruined what little mind he had left, but he's gonna live. And I'll have to explain what happened in *chingos* of reports, and then only about a dozen different times to the Town Council, the county DA, CBI investigators, maybe the state AG Hell, who knows who else. *Qué chingadera.*"

The tequila must've turned on a Spanish cuss word switch in López's tongue.

"Yeah, your job can be a bitch. I've noticed that."

He nodded and frowned. "It has its days, for sure."

I recognized sarcasm was not one of the cop's strengths.

Eight

The cop and I slammed another shot of tequila before he decided to return to his office. He said he needed to start on the paperwork that Delgado's suicide attempt had generated, and he still had to make his rounds before he called it a day. I doubted he would get anything done, but I let him go without encouraging him to stay. He'd probably fall asleep at his desk.

He'd loosened up considerably, and I almost choked on my beer when he called me "amigo" as he wobbled out of the bar. He was just another homie at that point, a neighborhood guy I might've run into back in the day when I roamed the Denver Chicano bars, loose and rowdy. A dude who would buy a round and expect two in return. Back then, we could've ended the night covering each other's six, or squaring off against one another because that's what the night called for. Except that Rob López wore a uniform. That was different, way different. Apparently, we'd bonded over Delgado's failed suicide attempt. Our frantic efforts to keep alive the washed-up writer, or whatever he was, had united us in a poor man's partnership, a union of unlikely first responders who didn't actually care if the victim lived or died. That was my take, upbeat as usual.

He'd made a favorable impression. I didn't hold it against him that he drank while on duty, nor that the veneer of law enforcement authority that covered his attraction to physical violence stretched tight and thin, ready to crack at a wrong word or crooked look from someone he'd arrested. I accepted López the way I found him. I had to. In my life, that's the way it had always been, the way it would always be. It was one reason I'd survived.

But until I knew exactly what had happened to Mat, I would assume anything was possible and suspect everyone in Melton, including the chief of police.

I ordered another Sand Creek Saloon hamburger and asked the bartender for directions to George's garage. While I waited for the burger, Werm the barfly approached me.

"Hey, there he is, the guy from Denver." His toothy smile couldn't have been more fake. "Remember me? We talked just the other day."

"Sure, I remember you. You were curious about the knot on my head."

"Uh, yeah, didn't mean to pry. You feelin' better?"

"I'm doing okay," I lied. "How about you?"

"Oh, hell, there ain't nothin' wrong with me, you know? I'm tip-top, hundred percent."

To prove the truth of his words, he chugged his beer and dramatically slammed the bottle on the bar.

"I heard you was talking to people about that missing kid, Montoya," he said. "That you're an investigator, or lawyer, somethin' like that."

"I'm looking for Mat Montoya, my cousin's boy, that's right. You know something that might help me?"

"Me? Nah. I don't even know the kid. I seen him around town, of course. I know his father, kind of. We don't hang out, don't take it wrong. He worked on my old van a while back, that's all. When I still had a license. But that's it."

"Where'd you see Mat? You mean, like walking around town, or at some event, what?"

"How about a beer? I'm kind of dry with all this talking."

I ordered him a beer. I didn't expect that he would provide me with anything I didn't already know but buying him a beer seemed like the thing I should do.

"So, tell me about the times you saw Mat," I said when he'd taken his first drink from the new bottle of beer.

"Well, I seen him all his life, basically. Ever since his momma and daddy brought him from the orphanage, or wherever they got him."

"Okay, sure. How about more recent? When's the last time you saw him?"

He sipped the beer and acted like he was thinking extra hard about an answer.

"Once," he said, "long before he run off, he was at that coffee shop with a girl, I think she's the doctor's kid. They was laughing and talking."

"Why's that stick in your head?"

"The truth? I've known Doc Cleary and his family forever. The Clearys and my family ain't exactly on friendly terms. It's about money, of course. Business. I leave all that to my sister. I was surprised that the girl had grown up and was hanging out with a boy, a Mexican kid at that."

"Something wrong with that?"

"Uh, I don't mean nothin'. I got nothin' against nobody, Mex or white or black. Just sayin' I didn't expect it, that's all. The woman, the doc's wife? She can be . . . picky, know what I mean?"

"That all you can tell me?"

"You only bought me a beer, mister. I said I don't know nothin' about that boy. And I ain't got nothin' against the Clearys. Don't get me wrong. It's business, that's all."

He walked away, mumbling about city assholes. He took the beer with him.

Freddy brought my hamburger. I asked for a glass of water to go with my lunch.

"Ignore that guy," Freddy said. "He's a trip but he's harmless. The only reason he can waste all day here in the bar is because of his monthly allowance from the Tanney Trust. He doesn't know anything else except this bar. Okay with me, but then I'm a bartender."

By the time I finished the food, the alcohol buzz faded, the incipient anxiety I'd carried from Denver calmed down a notch or two, and I calculated where I'd go next, if George agreed.

Freddy suggested I leave my truck parked and said it would take five minutes to walk to the garage. I asked him whether he knew Mat.

"Not really," the bartender said. "I mean, everyone in Melton knows everyone else, of course, but I can't say I really know the kid. He's eaten here a few times, usually with George or Essie, occasionally with someone from the school, one of his buddies. He never tried to buy a beer, which some of these kids will do. He's got a good rep as a smart kid."

"I hear that a lot," I said.

Outside the bar I decided I'd use the time to look closer at Melton. I quickly concluded there wasn't much else to see. I stopped my short hike at the corner of Main and Sherman streets, where I had a decent view of most of the town buildings. Ellen's Cozy Diner was closed, although a cardboard sign in the window assured the hungry residents of Melton that it was open. Next door, the coffee shop showed signs of life. A man and woman sat at the same table where Essie and I had talked with the teacher. A hundred yards north on Sherman, a gray church steeple towered over everything else. Behind the church sat a two-story brick building with an ornate pair of wooden doors. It must've been the school—elementary, middle, and high school all rolled into one. Back on Main, a secondhand store was open, but when I looked in the storefront window, I couldn't see anybody or anything inside. A liquor store had a handwritten sign in the doorway that read, "ring bell for service." At the end of Main, just before the street merged into the state highway, the gas station was busy with ranchers, farmers and what looked like construction workers filling their pickups.

George's garage didn't have any signs, but there was no mistaking what it was. Two trucks and a van were parked in front of the squat concrete building where they waited for attention. The van had a cracked windshield and one missing tire. Two bays were occupied by another truck and a bruised and tarnished Jeep.

George talked with a young man dressed in greasy overalls—his help, I assumed. They stood in a corner, half in shade and half in sunshine. I waved at George and he hustled to meet me. "Gus," he said. "Good to see you. I was gonna call, check in with what you've learned, if anything. I know it's only one day, but I was hoping, you know?"

"We should talk, George. I don't know much more than I did when I got here, but it's something."

"Sure, cuz. Let's go inside."

He took me to a side door that opened into a room that looked like the office of a man who would never admit he had an office. Greasy carburetors and corroded batteries were piled in one corner while stacks of invoices and receipts spread across a badly stained wooden desk. A simple wall calendar declared MONTOYA'S MOTORS—QUALITY SERVICE AND REPAIRS. The room smelled like oil and gasoline. I asked for some water, and he grabbed a plastic bottle from a small fingerprint-stained refrigerator and handed it to me.

I gave him my opinions about Delgado, the Clearys and O'Brien the teacher. I didn't hold back when I described my interaction with the Clearys and Delgado. I mentioned hatred, weirdness and con games.

He thought over what I'd said for several seconds. "This guy Delgado?" he finally asked. "He was a friend of Mat's? Doesn't sound like a person Mat would want to be around. Mat isn't careless about friendships. And this attempted suicide, what's that about? That doesn't have anything to do with Mat, does it?"

"We don't really know, not until we can talk to Delgado and get to the bottom of what his relationship with Mat actually was. At this point, I agree with Chief López. Wes Delgado had reached the end of his rope and gave up. He'd failed here in Melton, whatever he was trying to do, and I guess he didn't think he had any more options."

"I never did like that guy," George said. "Not even when every-body else around here treated him like a goddamned movie star. I'm one of the few who didn't give him any money, although he asked. More than once."

"He's not a likeable guy," I said.

"And the doctor and his wife? Jesus, what's going on? I'm on the Town Council with that guy. He's never come off like he and his wife did with you and Essie. I can't hardly believe it. You'd think they'd want to help. This is all fucked up."

"It was mostly the mother, acting out. But I don't doubt that the parents are the reason Yvonne and Mat broke up. Annie doesn't like Mexicans for whatever, and they yanked Yvonne away from Mat because of the way they feel. There could be some other rea-son, but only Mat and Yvonne would know it."

"You're not saying the Clearys know something about Mat's disappearance?"

"We don't know anything for sure, not yet. I wish I could give you more specific info, George. I really do."

He nodded.

"What do you think about the chief, López?"

"Rob? He's a cop, all you need to know," George answered. "That's his life. He grew up around here, but he came to us from Pueblo. He'd been a cop there. His job is easy, in my opinion; not many criminals in Melton. He does get into his work. A couple of times he got carried away, a little rough. Nothing serious, just a busted lip on a drunk, too much enthusiasm pulling over kids learning how to drive. That kind of thing. He does what he can, considering it's mostly him for law enforcement."

I finished by telling him that I should try to pick up Mat's trail somewhere other than Melton. I explained that I'd talk with Alicia and Connor again, and then, based on what they told me, I'd drive to Pueblo, hopefully with some clue where to look for Mat. I'd fol-low the leads I found there.

"Your plan assumes Mat headed to Pueblo. But he could be anywhere, right? Denver, Albuquerque. Hell, he might've split for Mexico."

"You're right, George. I'm guessing Pueblo because that's the only place Mat apparently ever talked about, the place where he had a good time, whatever that means. If Connor or Alicia give me a reason to think otherwise, I'll head off in a different direction. But for now, Pueblo is all we've got to go on."

He slumped in his chair. What I said hadn't made him feel any better about the chances for finding his missing son.

"Tell me, Gus," he said when he straightened up. "Honestly, now. You think you'll ever find him? You think I'll ever see Mat again?" I could barely hear him when he asked the questions whose answers he feared he'd regret, answers that would change his life forever.

The way he whispered messed with my thinking. For a second, dark images and emotions tumbled in my bruised head. I forced myself away from where I was headed and focused on George. He'd lost some hope, and my lack of good news about Mat had reinforced his gloom. So much for me giving him a happy ending.

"I just started on this, George." I had to be frank with my cousin, but I didn't want to cause him any unnecessary pain. "It's gonna take some time. Mat has a big head start on me. I'm playing catch-up. I'll keep at it until I find something definite. I can promise you that."

"You're willing to keep looking?"

"I am if you want me too. And I want to, George. Mat is family. I want to see him back home. I want you and him together again."

"I hope you can do it, Gus. I pray every night that Mat will come home. Now, I'll pray for you, too."

I left George at his garage, surrounded by his work and his fears. He'd instructed me to keep looking for Mat, and he approved of me traveling to Pueblo. When I was ready to leave Pueblo, I was to call him before I took the next step. Unless I found Mat, of course. Then I was to rush the boy home without delay. I promised I'd do exactly that. George tried to be upbeat, but it was a futile gesture. He was hurting, in pain, and I accepted that was the only rational feeling for a man in his shoes.

I headed straight to Essie's house. I didn't want to drive in the dark again on the lonely road, and I also wanted to set up another meeting with Mat's friend Connor, and Alicia.

This time the ride was uneventful. I didn't see any ghosts, Running Elk or otherwise, and I didn't have to drive in heavy darkness. I stayed on the road, made good time and arrived to share a plate of nachos with Essie and her mother.

Before we ate, I threw my dirty clothes into Essie's washing machine. She gave me an old pair of men's pants and a T-shirt to wear. She didn't explain why she had them, and I didn't ask.

The dull ache in my head had eased up and I vaguely realized that the dark shackle that had slowed me down for months had lessened its grip . . . not totally, not anywhere close to ending, but enough for me to admit that for the first time in a long time, I felt okay, considering.

≫ ≫ ≫

Felisa Montoya sat with Essie and me at the kitchen table. The nachos were gone but we continued our conversation.

"No game shows?" I asked. The old lady grinned and chuckled.

"Not yet, not the ones I like," she explained.

"She has her favorites," Essie said.

"Don't we all?" I said.

"A real busy day, right?" Essie said.

I went through my afternoon step by step, including the Wes Delgado mess. Then I explained what I'd gone over with George and that my next step was to drive to Pueblo. Essie and her mother agreed.

Before I could finish my recap, the mother uttered, "Mat told me that he liked the Riverwalk in Pueblo. Called it his spot."

"Really?" I said.

"When was that, mother?" Essie said. "When did you talk with Mat about Pueblo?"

Felisa shrugged. Her thin gray hair vibrated with her every move. The wrinkles around her mouth and eyes squirmed when she talked, and the loose skin at her jowls and neck shook like feathers in the wind.

"How do I know when?" she asked. "I don't know what today is, forget about when I talked with my grandson. But it happened. He sat right there where Mr. Cortez is sitting and said to me that the Pueblo Riverwalk was one of his favorite places to chill. That's what he said, don't you know? 'Chill.' I always thought Pueblo was too hot."

"His name's Corral, mom. Gus Corral. Not Cortez."

"What did I say? Didn't I say Corral? You're Alejandra's boy, no? I always liked Alejandra. Didn't care that much for Esteban, but Alejandra was an angel."

I wanted to thank her for praising my mother, and I wanted to ask her why she didn't like my father, but Essie stopped all conversation when she stood up and announced that her mother was going to the front room to watch TV.

"Sorry about that," Essie said when she returned from setting up her mother for the evening. "She gets confused, like a lot of older folks. Some things stick in her head, the smallest detail, while other things, stuff that just happened yesterday, get lost."

"Well, she remembers my parents. That's good, no?"

"Yeah, I guess. I wouldn't take too seriously that she thinks Mat talked to her about Pueblo. That could've been one of her dreams, or maybe she saw something like it on a TV show. It's been a long time since Mat had a conversation with my mother."

"It's interesting, though. There are places to hang out for kids along the river in Pueblo. It's worth checking out. I would've gone there anyway, whether your mother mentioned it or not."

"I suppose." Essie finished with a loud sigh.

She carried the same weight as George. The close-knit Montoya family put on a strong front, but the strain of Mat's absence had exposed the cracks.

"I'll find someone in Pueblo who remembers Mat," I said. "That might be all we need. One name, one person who remembers something Mat said that will open this up for us."

"If only that can happen. I hope you do find that person, Gus, so that we can get on with our lives. God, listen to me. Is that selfish of me?"

"No, of course not."

"And I worry about George. He has to move forward. He's paying a heavy price, emotionally. You know what I mean, Gus?"

"Absolutely. We'll get some answers, I know that. It's only a matter of time, and for me to do what I need to do to find those answers. I'll keep at it until I find Mat."

"Thank you, Gus. I know you'll do your best. I hope it's enough."

Nine

That night I called Corrine. My older sister had become my go-to-person for honest answers and necessary advice, and I needed to bounce a few things off her. I wasn't always comfortable with our relationship, but I'd learned, the hard way, that I should listen to her and do what she suggested, no matter how much it cost me in terms of sibling rivalry points. She'd saved my ass more than once. It was as simple as that.

"It doesn't look good for finding Mat," she said when I'd finished my *Reader's Digest* version of my short time in eastern Colorado. "To be missing this long, without any word? He's either gone forever, hurt or even worse. I feel for George. His kids are really all he has. It's a sad job, Gus. You may have to deliver bad news. I'm sorry I got you involved."

"Don't say that. I can do some good. Give George and Essie closure, like they say. An ending, any ending, is better than what they have now. These cousins of ours are strong people, but I can see they're wearing out. I want to help."

"I wouldn't say *any* ending would be better."

"Yeah, you may be right. I'll do what I can. Maybe it'll do some good."

"Okay, Gus."

Here it comes, I thought.

"But don't get yourself in too deep. You're not in the best shape, we both know that. Before you go on to Pueblo, maybe you ought to come back to Denver for a few days. Charge your batteries, brother. See if anything's happening at your office. Don't overdo it. You know how you are."

I let a second tick away, as if I were thinking over Corrine's suggestion. "No, I wouldn't feel good about stopping now. I'll keep on until there's nothing left to check. You wouldn't stop now, would you?"

I could almost see her shaking her head. "Guess not. If you think you can handle it, then you should keep at it. I didn't expect anything else. You've always been stubborn."

"Committed. Not stubborn."

"Ha! You should be committed, for sure."

We both laughed. I reassured her that I was feeling better than when I'd left Denver, and I explained that I'd only be two or three days in Pueblo. Then I'd either go back to Melton and finish up with George or follow Mat's trail if I found anything.

"One other thing, Gus."

"What's that?" Over the years I'd learned that Corrine's *one other thing* often was a half-dozen or more other things . . . important things that usually meant I had to be extra cautious or work extra hard.

"The changes since your accident."

Corrine called my run-in with the baseball client an accident, but there was nothing accidental about the assault on my head with the Louisville Slugger.

"Yeah, I know. I'm not all here, not all back yet. I know that." Damn, the entire Chicano population of Denver knew that.

"No, something else. You can become belligerent, aggressive, without thinking things through. I've noticed it comes on when you feel extra stressed, which is a lot of the time. Before you get defensive, listen to me. I'm only saying this to clue you in. You haven't done anything that needs correcting, but you should be aware of what might happen if you lose it. Who knows how far you will go if you slip over that edge I'm talking about? And that's different for you, a side I'm not used to. Just be careful, that's all."

She was right. It was something I'd seen in myself that I didn't recognize. If I felt boxed in, I'd start thinking about options to immediately get out of the box, and those options often included violence. Sometimes it felt like losing complete control was only a push away.

"I'm always careful, sis. No way am I going to 'lose it,' as you put it."

"I'm only trying to help, Gus."

"And I appreciate it. I hear you. I'll maintain."

She grunted as though I stretched an obvious point.

"So, anything stick out from what I've told you about the people of Melton?" I asked.

"Let's say that this isn't simply a runaway situation," she answered. "Let's consider the worst possible scenario."

"Mat's dead?" I hesitated, but the words had to be spoken.

"Yes. Where's that lead us?"

"What's the cause of death? Accident? Wouldn't somebody contact the family?"

"When he's identified. But that assumes his body is found. What if he's lying out in a gulley somewhere? He might never be found."

"Okay, that's one outcome."

"A sad one, but not the worst."

"You mean, what if he's dead and it wasn't an accident?" I asked.

"Right."

"But there's no reason to think that. One thing I've learned is that everybody likes Mat. Or at least admires him. That's what they all say."

"Not everyone likes Mat."

"The Clearys, the doctor and his wife?"

"Yes. Maybe they wanted to make sure that their daughter absolutely stayed away from Mat. Forever."

"You do go for the dark, Corrine. And the Clearys may be prejudiced, but I can't see them hurting Mat. If you met them face-to-face and talked with them, you'd see what I mean. No doubt they're capable of some shady shit, but I can't picture them harming someone directly, in a physical way."

"I'm just throwing stuff out there. That's why you called, ain't it? I'm sure you didn't just want to catch up on Northside *chisme*."

"Yeah, yeah. You know me too well."

"How about this Delgado character? He sounds like he could do something extreme. Doesn't trying to kill himself make him the prime suspect?"

"He's weird enough, for sure. But, again, what's the motive? According to Delgado, he and Mat were on good terms. I didn't get any sense that he would hurt Mat. And nothing stands out as a potential motivation."

"You're probably right. But his motive could be connected to the missing backpack."

"True. Delgado flipped out when he discovered that Mat's pack had been stolen. He took it harder than I'd expect. It wasn't his, after all. Yet, he almost cried when he figured someone had taken it."

"Maybe he used it to hide something? Money? Drugs?"

"Could be. Or maybe Mat gave him something in the backpack, and he couldn't deal with the fact that he'd lost it. I should talk to Delgado again, and I will, when he's ready."

"Yeah, that'll be an interesting conversation. Let's hope that you and I are only complicating what is simply a teenaged runaway situation."

"That's our MO, isn't it?"

"Maybe. And now I've got to ask . . ."

"George?"

"Yes. Any chance he had something to do with whatever's happened to Mat?"

"I've thought about it, of course. Much as I hated to. There are a few red flags. People keep telling me he and Mat had a troubled relationship. Everyone except Essie. Arguments, fights. I figured Mat's uneasy connection to his father was probably the main reason he kept running off. Plus, typical teenager rebellion. And the adoption thing. Mat's at the age where he wants answers."

"Like who his biological parents were, why'd they give him up? That stuff?"

"Right. He might be looking for his parents, and he doesn't want George or anyone else to get in his way. That's easy to believe. Throw it all together and you have a dysfunctional family in the making."

"But not enough to think George might've harmed Mat?"

"I don't see it. Maybe I don't want to. But George is really upside down about Mat. He doesn't come off as a bad father or a cruel man. He's complicated, dealing with issues from his time in combat, but he appears to have all that under control, or at least in a holding pattern. And he hired me to look for Mat. Doesn't gibe with him trying to cover up something."

"No, it doesn't. Unless . . ."

"I know. Unless George is putting on a show to throw me off."

"Dang," Corrine muttered. "Who's on the dark side now?"

"I know, I know. I can't believe what we're talking about, but I have to at least think about it, don't I?"

"Afraid so, Gus. Comes with the territory."

Corrine hung up after I promised I would keep her in the loop about what I was doing and where I was going.

That night, as I lay in Essie's guest bedroom and once again listened to the rain and thunder roll over the plains, I rewound my conversation with Corrine and went over it again. I picked out the answers I'd change and what other questions I should ask. The last image in my head before I fell asleep was the strange figure I'd encountered in the darkness the first night I was in Melton. I hadn't told Corrine about that experience.

The next morning, after breakfast, Essie and I drove to the Bannon ranch to meet Connor and Alicia. The plan was that George would drop off Alicia on his way to work, and Connor would be waiting for us. Essie told me that the boy worked and lived on the ranch for most of the summer.

"Leroy is Connor's uncle," she said. "I wouldn't doubt that one day Connor will own the ranch, if he wants it. Not too many kids stay here after they finish high school."

We were almost at the ranch when my cousin asked, "Why investigator, Gus? It's a peculiar profession. Not the first thing that comes to mind when talking about possible careers."

"It's different, I'll give you that. I kind of fell into it. The simple answer is that with my record, it's one of the few meaningful jobs I can hold. If I'm ever convicted of another felony, I'll lose my license, but my record didn't get in the way of me getting a PI license in the first place. I went through a full background check and a couple of intense interviews with ex-cops, but ultimately the state gave me a license."

"Yeah, okay," Essie said. "I get that. But, investigator?"

"My lawyer, Luis Móntez, gave me a job when I was released from prison. I stuck with it after he retired. Now, it's all I know to do."

"I've heard of Móntez. He's kind of famous, even in Melton. Good man."

"I agree. He's come through for me more than once."

"And you were injured in your last case? No second thoughts?"

"I like the work, believe it or not. It's usually not so dramatic or life-threatening, but I feel like I'm accomplishing something, even in the boring times. Mostly, I serve court papers, interview witnesses, photograph two-timing husbands on a date with their lovers. Occasionally, I testify in court. My last case, working for the ballplayer, was different, and that's why I got hurt. I should've seen it coming."

"Maybe Melton can be good for you, especially after we find Mat."

"Unless someone comes after me with a bat. It'll be good to feel like my old self. Some people might doubt that's an improvement."

Essie laughed, and for a second the strain disappeared from her face. That's when I saw the obvious, something I'd missed because it was right in front of me. My cousins, Essie and George, and my sisters, Corrine and Max . . . physically, there was no doubt that these people were related. They could've passed as four siblings from the same set of parents. The set of the eyes, the ever-present half-smile, half-frown, dark thick hair. I included myself in the group. Ever since I was a kid, I'd been told that Corrine could've been my twin. Whatever the relationship, the Montoyas from Melton and the Corrals from Denver shared blood, and more.

We finished the drive with me asking Essie if Mat had any enemies and Essie assuring me that Mat was a popular guy, well-liked, even respected by adults.

"Except the Clearys," I pointed out.

"Don't get me started on them. That scene came out of left field. But yeah, not everyone likes Mat, apparently. You don't think they did something to Mat, do you?"

"Covering all the bases," I said. "If Mat had a serious rival or adversary, then I'd investigate that person, just in case. But there's no one?"

"The only person I can think of is Connor, of all people, and it's nothing. Like Susan said, Connor is more like Mat's brother than a friend. They do everything together. The only reason I mention him is because for a while Connor was mad at Mat because Mat dated Yvonne Cleary. Connor had been her boyfriend until they broke up. Then, about a month later, Mat and Yvonne became a couple. Connor sulked and wouldn't talk to Mat, but he got over it. Mat and Yvonne split, and Yvonne and Connor tried to be a couple again, then they finally ended their relationship. High school romance, right? It's not like Mat stole Yvonne from Connor. Mat had nothing to do with Connor and Yvonne separating. Mat told me that Connor was okay, and then Mat and Yvonne flamed out, so it was all good between the two boys. You remember what being a teenager was like, don't you, Gus? That's what was going on with Mat and Connor."

"I remember some of my high school years. Most of it I've tried to forget."

The ranch came into view and I parked in the same spot I'd used before. Alicia and Connor were waiting on the sunny front porch of the ranch house, where Leroy Bannon's housekeeper had set up coffee, juice and blueberry muffins.

Mat's best friend and sister didn't try to conceal their excitement. They were eager to tell Essie and me that Mat had sent them a text message. Essie rushed to look at the message on the teenagers' phones.

HEY, WHATS UP? IM ON THE ROAD STILL. BE HOME SOON.

"When did you get this?" I asked. "You each got the same message?"

"Yes," Connor said. "Mine came in this morning."

"Mine, too," Alicia said. "About a half hour ago."

"You're sure it's from Mat?" Essie asked.

"Who else?" Alicia answered. "It's his number. His ID came up. I'm so glad he finally contacted us."

"Did you call him?" I asked.

"As soon as I got his text," Connor said.

"Me too," Alicia added.

"No answer, just voicemail, so I texted him, too," Connor said. "He'll call me, sooner or later. That's the way he is."

"I did the same," Alicia said. "He'll get back to one of us."

"You show this to your father?" I asked.

"Not yet. He'd already dropped me off. Mat's text came in while I waited for Connor. I was going to call Dad when you drove up."

"Call him now, Alicia," Essie said. "It's what George has been waiting for."

The next hour was a blur of joyful energy coming from Essie and Alicia. After the call to George, and after Essie gave the good news to Bannon, I drove Alicia and Essie to Essie's house. The two laughed and talked all the way. They told one Mat story after another as they remembered the good times they'd shared. At the house, Felisa clapped her hands and did a dance step with her walker when she read Mat's message. Alicia announced that she had to spread the good news to her friends. Essie talked about a celebration dinner, and she and her mother started planning for a major party at the house. She intended to invite George and Alicia, of course, Connor and Bannon, and the teacher, O'Brien. And me.

"Maybe you ought to save the party for when Mat actually comes home," I said.

"Oh, we'll party then, don't worry about that, Gus. And you and your sisters will be invited to that party, too. You have to come for that. Promise?"

"Of course. Corrine and Max will kill me if I don't bring them. You can count on all three of us being here."

"So, you'll stay tonight?"

I begged off, again, and this time I convinced Essie that I should hit the road. She relented, finally, only because I told her I needed to get to my work in Denver. She understood that reason.

It took several more minutes to say my goodbyes to Essie and Felisa, who insisted on reinviting me to their party. Then they found it necessary to pack sandwiches, candy bars and potato chips in a cardboard box for my trip. When the box was ready, I gave the two women another hug and threw my backpack and the food box in the truck.

They stood at the edge of the street as I pulled away. They shouted goodbye and thank you and were still waving at me when I turned the corner and I couldn't see Essie's house in my rearview mirror.

I drove the pickup to Main Street, where I topped off the gas tank, stopped at George's garage, confirmed I was leaving Melton and told George to call me when Mat showed up.

George Montoya was a different man. The gray shadow that had followed him had disappeared. He looked ten years younger. He asked me to give Corrine and Max a hug for him when I made it to Denver. I assured him I would.

His final words to me were simple: "Thank you."

I started to say I hadn't really done anything and that Mat was on his way home through no effort on my part. But instead, I gave my cousin a handshake and a pat on the back that might've been a hug. I promised to see him again when Mat's homecoming would be celebrated. Then I drove back through Main Street until I was at the intersection where I had the choice of left to the Pueblo highway or right to the Denver freeway. I put on my sunglasses, turned up the country music on the radio and headed to Pueblo.

Ten

When Corrine and I were kids, the southern Colorado town of Pueblo was where we escaped whatever crazy *pendejadas* we were dealing with in Denver's Northside. There was a stretch of five or six years when our mother would periodically itch to take a break from everything, including our father and the frantic Denver pace. Often, she'd detect a restlessness in Corrine or me, and she'd know something was going on with us, and not in a good way. We were hell-raisers, always on the verge of chaos and anarchy. In our best interests, and hers, too, I'm sure, she'd decide it was time to leave. She'd scheme with various relatives who lived in what used to be called the Steel City, and one day my mother, sisters and yours truly would pack bags of clothes and take off before sunrise to visit aunts, uncles and cousins we knew from stories our parents told us when they talked about their youth and the "old days."

Corrine and I looked forward to those trips, usually at the end of summer. Maxine was too young to appreciate what was going on, but she traveled with us anyway, oblivious to what Corrine and I considered a big deal.

We were intimidated, in a good way, by the Pueblo cousins, boys and girls. They dressed cool, in styles taken from movies and magazines. They talked in jazzy slang and half-Spanish, half-English phrases. They knew the words to all the latest songs, the newest dance steps and the life histories of Latino singers and musicians. They were upfront about their Mexican heritage and cultural history. They were too young to have lived through the Chicano Movement, but they were throwbacks to those heady times of Chicano soul and pride, days that old-timers like my lawyer Móntez reminisced about, days that stuck in the previous generation's psyches, days that influenced their entire lives. There were kids like the Pueblo tribe in Denver, of course, but we weren't related to the Denver versions, and the Pueblo breed had a low-key, smooth facade that Denver lacked. Every interaction in Denver—party, dance, baptism—could end up in an argument or a fight, or worse, all between brown-skinned kids. In the Northside, it seemed that Corrine and I constantly threw down with someone over petty hassles that made sense only in the scarred world of Chicano Denver. In Pueblo, the biggest arguments were over who rode shotgun when we cruised the neon streets in a waxed and polished set of wheels driven by one of the older cousins.

Hot and dry Pueblo in the summer meant sticky asphalt, still air that buzzed with overheated insects and mellow brilliant nights. During the drive from Melton, I thought about our summer trips, but I couldn't remember one distinct event or occasion that should've stuck in my memory bank. Instead, I recalled generic lazy days lounging in the backyard of a patched frame house and cool evenings sitting next to the muddy river while R&B, hip-hop and oldies played in the background. I vaguely pictured dark-haired and dark-skinned girls who laughed at my T-shirts and black tennis shoes, but who easily slipped into my arms for slow dancing and heavy breathing. The memories coalesced into a film clip from my adolescence that flickered and flared.

I knew it was crazy to think that I would find anything like the Pueblo of my youth, but the movie scenes I'd pinned together kept me entertained for some of the three-hour journey from Melton to Pueblo. The rest of the time I organized what I knew about the runaway mystery of Mat Montoya.

My bruised brain strongly suggested that I should tell Essie and George that I doubted Mat had sent the text messages to Alicia and Connor, but I didn't have the heart to follow through. I didn't want to bring down the euphoria and spoil the celebration. I also didn't have anything concrete on which to base my hunch . . . except those text messages didn't feel right. If my feeling was correct, the celebrating would not last long. Someone had tried to throw me off the trail. At least, that was one scenario, and it could easily have been only a product of my paranoia. In the cab of my pickup, on the long monotonous highway to Pueblo, I tossed those thoughts around like tumbling dice. Before I saw an exit sign for Pueblo, I fell into a bleak, grainy mood.

I took the exit, pulled over and parked in the shade of a Mineral Palace Park tree. I would've bet a paint job for my truck that when someone from out of state thought of Colorado, they didn't envision Pueblo. It had little resemblance to Aspen or Boulder or Denver, in people, history or culture.

I couldn't see them from the park, but I knew the old steel mill smokestacks poked over the southern edge of the town, and that in many ways the city still gave off an independent working-class vibe. Gun ownership was high, elected officials ran the risk of recall elections if they wandered too far left and the city had a higher crime rate than the national average. Added to the mix was the fact that several Medal of Honor recipients were from Pueblo, and the city was known as the Home of Heroes. And, like a cherry on top, the Mafia owned a chapter or two of Pueblo history.

I drove through the downtown streets: Santa Fe, Union, Main, First. No real skyline, although it was obvious that the city planners were working on the city's image. The Riverwalk, along the recon-figured Arkansas River, provided an escape from the notorious Pueblo heat with restaurants, boutique shops, bars and public art. I drove over a bridge and saw groups of people walking along the river while pedal boats and gondolas cruised the easy-going man-made branches of the main river.

I didn't have to think too long to assume that when Mat ended up in Pueblo, he didn't hop in one of the gondolas with the tourists. I had to look for the hidden Pueblo where runaways, druggies and fugitives gathered, where someone on the skids might find a place to sleep for a night or two.

I did a quick search on my phone and came up with the address for the place mentioned by Susan O'Brien, The Rising Sun, billed as a shelter for homeless youth. Google also informed me that Toni Marriot, Ph.D., had served as the Director of The Rising Sun for the past eighteen months.

I grabbed a chicken sandwich from a drive-through fast food joint, then drove to the center of the town, a few blocks from the Riverwalk. The revamping of Pueblo hadn't reached this section of the city. Peeling paint, cardboard-covered windows and exposed brick made the buildings here look overused and tired. A half-dozen men and women congregated on a corner near a pair of shopping carts loaded with what most people would consider junk. A torn tent drooped in the afternoon heat against one of the faded brick walls. Off to one side, a hand-painted sign in a store-front window announced that The Rising Sun was open. I parked and made my way to the shelter.

I opened a gray metal door and the smells of marijuana, sweat and cigarettes immediately hit me. I walked into a gray room whose walls were covered with posters and stickers. Scuff marks and coffee stains dotted the hardwood floor.

Several gray folding chairs were scattered around the room. Along one wall, a counter with large pantry doors supported a half-empty coffee pot, about a dozen coffee mugs and the remnants of a chocolate cake. A curtained doorway near the back of the room appeared to lead to another room, or maybe an exit.

A pair of scrawny girls, about Alicia's age I guessed, huddled in a corner, whispering and giggling. I waved at the girls, but they ignored me. I was about to ask if there was someone in charge of the place, when a woman walked through the curtain.

"Can I help you?" she asked.

She rubbed her hands together as though she was cold, which made no sense, but what bothered me was her frown. She didn't look happy to see me. She wore black jeans, a gray shirt and a pair of gray sneakers that had white blotches. Her short brown hair framed a soft-looking face and dull gray eyes.

"Hello," I said, in the friendliest tone I could dredge up. "I hope you can. My name's Gus Corral. You must be Toni Marriot?"

She didn't respond, not with a word or a nod of her head.

"I'm here on behalf of the family of Mat Montoya. They asked me to find out what I can about Mat. He's..."

"A runaway? Really?" She smiled at the girls, who continued to giggle. "You found the runaway place. And you think your boy's been through The Rising Sun? Good for you."

"So, you can help me?" I asked, not sure what to expect.

She picked up one of the coffee mugs and took a sip of whatever was in the cup. "People just don't learn." She shook her head and put the cup back on the counter. The golden hoops hanging from her ear lobes jiggled and flashed.

"Learn what?" I asked.

"That I don't give out information about any of the kids who come through here. I don't care where they're from, how long they've been on the road or what kind of trouble they're running from. Or who's asking the questions. I don't do it. These kids need to trust me if I'm gonna help them. There's no trust if I talk about them to anybody who shows up. Kids know if they make it here, they can relax, rest up, get off the streets for a night or two. No one's gonna give them up."

"I understand, but I'm only . . ."

"Not unless you have a court order," she quickly added. "That's different. I take it you don't have that all-important piece of paper?" She rubbed her hands together again.

"I don't have a court order, and I'm not asking you to betray any confidences. I just need to know if Mat's been through here recently. Or if he's here now, maybe upstairs? That's all. It'll mean a lot to his family. They are very worried about him."

"Can't help you. Sorry." She smiled and folded her arms across her chest.

I tried a few more times, but she wouldn't cooperate. It didn't matter how I asked, she wasn't going to answer any questions about Mat or anyone else. My head flipped a switch and I started to think about other ways I could pry information from Toni Marriot, Ph. D. I had first-hand knowledge that a baseball bat could be very convincing, and I also knew that it wouldn't be hard to hurt the woman without any weapon in my hands. I stopped my train of thought when I imagined blood squirting from her nose. I decided I should leave before I lost my withering patience altogether.

I told Marriot that she could text me if she changed her mind, and I gave her my cell number. She didn't write it down. I walked out without swearing at her.

Back on the street, I stood near my pickup trying to come up with my next move. *How could I persuade Marriot that it was okay to talk to me about Mat? What did I have to do to convince her that it was in Mat's best interests that she give me whatever she could about Mat? Who else could I talk to about Mat?*

I heard a shout from behind me. I turned and saw two of the homeless men rolling in the street. They piled over one another like a pair of dusty bears trying to make love. Punches were thrown, but nothing connected. Curses rang out from each man, along with threats to break a leg or cut an eyeball. Grunts and whistles followed the threats. Meanwhile, the rest of the group ignored the thrashing pair. With a flurry of kicks, one of the men finally broke free from the wrestling match. He staggered to the tent and fell through the opening. The other man grabbed a bottle from one of his friends and chugged a long, sloppy drink.

I decided the wild bunch might be a source of information. *No worse than the damn director, right?*

I walked in their direction, ready to offer money or booze for information. Before I made it to the group, however, one of the girls I'd seen in the shelter emerged from the doorway and hollered at me.

"Hey, mister," she shouted. "I know someone who can tell you all about Mat."

She was skinny and pale. Black hair with red streaks, black lipstick and black clothes completed the cliché. I wanted to tell her that she should find a shower, and didn't she have any respect for herself?

"What do you know about Mat?" I asked.

She giggled. "Don't get personal, mister." She giggled again.

"I don't understand," I said.

She didn't answer. Her eyes rolled backwards, and her knees vibrated. She started to say something, but the words wouldn't fall from her mouth.

I was wasting my time with the giggling teenager. I turned away from the girl and headed toward the homeless group. What did it say about my investigative skills if my only options for information were a rowdy band of homeless drunks or a spaced-out wolf girl?

"You're from Melton, ain't you?" She finally managed to speak.

What she said stopped me. She knew about Melton, which meant she knew something about Mat, and that was enough for me to talk to her.

"And who are you? What's your name? How do you know Mat? Where is he?"

My questions shot out in rapid fire, and the girl backed up against the wall as though she wanted to duck out of the way.

"Take it easy, mister," she said. She found her breath and strung several words together. "I heard you asking Toni about Mat. She don't know nothing. My friend, Alex, can help you. He and Mat know each other. I can take you to Alex. Make an introduction." She paused, smiled. "If you make it worth my time."

For a hot second I thought about shaking her until she told me all she knew about Mat. Instead, I pulled a twenty from my wallet. "You give me something that helps me find Mat, and this is yours."

She nodded her head like a bobble doll with a loose spring. "Alex knows stuff. But he won't talk to you for free, mister. That's the way it is."

"Where is this friend of yours?"

"He crashes over at the Sangre. He's got a room."

"The Sangre? Blood? What is that?"

"The hotel. The Sangre de Cristo Hotel, over on Main. Jeez, you don't know much about Pueblo, do you?"

I knew that Colorado had a mountain range named for the blood of Christ, and that Pueblo had an art gallery and event center also named for the same blood. The event center was only a few blocks to the east; the mountain range peaked through low-flying clouds to the southwest. Never would've guessed the hotel. But it made sense that the lost child trying to get to my money would offer to take me to a downtown hotel named for blood. Made sense to me, at least.

"What's the story on your friend, Alex?" I asked. "What do I need to know about him?"

"Gawd, mister. You ask too many questions. He's just a guy. He knows a lot of people, he gets around. You want to meet him, or not? I don't want to answer any more questions. And I got things to do. I'm just trying to help, and you givin' me the third degree."

"Show me the way. We walking?"

"Yeah, it's not far. Won't take long." She started up the street, and I stuck close to her, matching her speedy rhythm.

"You never told me your name," I said.

"That's right, I didn't. You can call me Jeannie."

"Okay, Jeannie. Not that you asked, but you can call me Gus."

"Yeah, whatever."

The longer we walked, the speedier she set the pace. Half a block from The Rising Sun we were practically jogging.

"What's the rush?" I said.

"I told you. I got things to do. And Alex gets impatient if he has to wait. He's like me. Got to keep moving."

"He knows we're coming?"

She stopped. "Of course. I called him when I heard you ask for Mat. I knew Toni wouldn't tell you nothing. Alex don't care, but I needed to make sure he would talk to you. One thing I've learned, Alex don't like surprises. He said to bring you to his place."

She returned to her jog. I followed her through the grimy entrance of the Sangre de Cristo Hotel.

Eleven

No one stood behind the large wooden check-in counter. I heard a telephone ringing. The old-fashioned bell stopped suddenly. An eerie silence settled over the hotel's entranceway. Jeannie walked past the desk and motioned for me to keep up.

We rode a noisy elevator to the second floor, then walked down a dark hallway decorated with a mangy carpet and stained walls. Before we knocked, the door to room 212 opened, and a short man with buzzed hair, red pants and no shirt waved at us and stepped back into the room. He held a cell phone to his ear and snorted occasionally until he ended the call and focused his attention on me. He looked Central American, like an indigenous refugee from someplace south of Mexico, someone who knew how to cross borders unseen and travel fast and light, a man who knew how to survive.

A dresser, three chairs, a small table and a bed took up most of the space in the small room, and I felt cramped and hemmed in. Steamy air from an open window circulated like heavy cotton.

Jeannie held out her hand, and I gave her the twenty.

"What you got for me today, Jeannie?" the man said while he looked me over. "You're always with a surprise. *Qué chica.*"

Jeannie giggled. She moved to Alex's side and kissed him on the cheek. "This guy's looking for Mat. He'll pay you for info. Remember Mat? The smart one."

"Einstein?" He sounded surprised. "You looking for Einstein?" He asked, his eyes roaming over my jeans, shirt and boots, then finally my face. Sweat glistened across his bare chest. He drank from a can of beer sitting on the table.

"If you mean Mat Montoya, yeah, I'm looking for him," I said. "His family's worried. They haven't heard from him for several weeks. They asked me to help find him."

He set down the beer and lit a cigarette. "You related? *Familia*?"

"His father is my cousin. I'm from Denver."

"*¿Primos, eh?* And they asked you? Why they do that?"

I didn't appreciate the interrogation. I wanted to get to the point and then leave the stuffy room, but I played along with his game. One of Corrine's pieces of advice was to be patient with people. Patience was never one of my strong points, but I held back and worked out how to respond to the short Indian. I figured he wanted to impress Jeannie, although I couldn't think of a good reason to do that.

"I'm an investigator. Looking for people is one of the things I do. Plus, as I said, Mat's part of my family. His father is concerned. He just wants to know that Mat is okay." I paused to let that sink in. "Jeannie told me you're a man who might help, that you're the guy in Pueblo who knows what's going on. Are you that man?"

Jeannie shook her head, but she didn't say anything about my slight exaggeration of what she'd told me.

"Investigator?" he asked. "Like a cop?"

"No. I'm not police. Just a guy looking for a lost relative, Matías Montoya. Mat."

"We called him Einstein," Jeannie said. "He was off the grid with his smarts. Guy knew about everything. I liked him, I thought he . . ."

"He hasn't been around for a while," Alex interrupted. "I think the last time we saw him was like three months ago, something like that."

I pulled my wallet from my back pocket and dug out another twenty-dollar bill.

Alex shook his head. "No. You don't pay me. I don't know anything to help you. Mat's not around here, and he hasn't been for a while. That's all I know. *Nada más.*"

"You sure?" I asked. I still held the money.

He nodded at the twenty. "That won't change what I already told you, guy. I got nothing to tell you."

I shrugged. "Mat's been missing about a month. You didn't see him a month ago?"

"Well, it could " Jeannie started to answer, but Alex interrupted her again.

"No. It was more than that, three months, maybe four. Beginning of summer at least. So, no, we can't help you."

He looked at Jeannie in a way that dared her to contradict him. She turned and walked to the open window, where she stared out onto the quiet Pueblo streets.

I returned the twenty to my wallet and the wallet to my pants.

"Okay. I'll be on my way."

Jeannie twisted her torso to look at me. She shrugged and headed to the door. "I've gotta go," she said.

Alex nodded and then turned to me. "You be careful out there. . . . There's some bad men out there. Pueblo ain't a friendly town."

I followed Jeannie out of the room to the hallway.

Behind me, Alex said, "I'll see you later. At the Center. You got it?"

"Yeah, yeah," Jeannie answered. "Later."

Jeannie wouldn't look at me in the elevator.

"That was a bust," I said. "You said that guy could help. What's going on?"

She shook her head. "You have to ask him."

"I paid you twenty bucks because you said Alex would know something. You owe me twenty dollars of information."

My attempt at patience was over. It had lasted longer than I expected.

"Uh-uh. No. That's not right."

The elevator door opened, and she scurried out. I grabbed her by the elbow, glared into her face and repeated my words, "You owe me."

She tried to jerk free from my grip, but she couldn't do it. I twisted her arm.

"I owe you shit! Let me go." She looked around, but there was no one else. The first floor of the hotel was still empty and dark. "Look. I don't know what the hell is up with Alex. He's acting strange. You're going to have to get it from him, whatever he knows. Now, let me go. You're hurting me. Or I start screaming 'rape.'"

That's when I focused on the bruises and scars on her arms. A few of the marks looked like burns. I released my hold on the girl and realized what I'd done. I stepped back from her.

"I'm sorry," I said. "I shouldn't have done that. I won't hurt you. I'm worried about Mat. And I think you are, too. Your friend Alex is in the way. He got me worked up."

I rubbed my sore head and felt the blood pulsing close to the surface of my scalp. I regretted that I hadn't taken a painkiller before I wandered into The Rising Sun.

"Let's get some coffee or something. We can talk. I won't hurt you," I repeated. "I promise."

She rubbed her elbow. "I've had worse."

She shook her arm and rolled her shoulders. I could almost touch the sadness coming from her. I recognized the hurt and something else: resignation. Acceptance.

"No big thing," she said.

"You want coffee?"

She hesitated, then nodded. "You can buy me a sandwich and tea at the place around the corner."

The coffee shop was three streets away, closer to the Riverwalk. I thought for a second that she was taking me on another wild goose chase, but we ended up in the Steel Unicorn, a sandwich and pastry joint whose half-dozen customers appeared to be no older than Jeannie, and just as disheveled and grungy. For the second time that day, the pungent smell of body odor mixed with marijuana hit me when I walked through the door.

At the counter, Jeannie ordered chai tea and a sprouts and avocado wrap. I settled for coffee. The drinks were quickly served, and we sat at a shaky table in a corner of the shop. I waited for a few minutes while Jeannie sipped her hot tea.

"Mat was here a month ago, wasn't he?" I asked when the food was brought to our table.

She swallowed a bite of the wrap, then nodded her head. "He blew into town and hung around for a few days. He spent a lot of time with Alex, so I didn't talk to him much."

"Your friend Alex is a flake, to say the least. Makes me think he had something to do with Mat's disappearance. Why did Alex lie?"

"Got me, mister. People do fucked up shit, no reason. All I know is Alex and Mat had something going on. They always did."

"Something like what?"

She wouldn't look me in the face. "I don't want to cause trouble. And I'm no snitch."

"And I'm not a cop, so whatever you tell me stays with me. I just want to find Mat, that's all."

"Mat used to help Alex with stuff. Know what I mean?"

"No, I don't. Explain."

She surveyed the other people in the shop, looking for eavesdroppers I assumed. "Alex's into shady business."

"*Really?*"

"Screw you."

"You mean drugs?"

"Well, some of that. But other stuff. He works with people from Texas. I've seen these guys go up to his room, late at night usually. Alex always gets rid of me when they're in town. They look mean, that's all I know."

"Texas? How do you know that?"

"I got eyes, mister. They usually show up driving trucks or vans. And the plates are Texas. And they sound like Texas assholes."

"White guys?"

"Yeah. And Mexicans, even a black guy."

"You said Alex is into other stuff. Like what?"

"Keep it down. You're making me nervous."

"Okay, okay." I lowered my tone. "What else?"

"It's about people crossing the border. That much Mat told me once. You know . . . illegals and that kind of border shit. I've seen women in the vans, kids even. That's all I know."

"Where did you see this? Here in Pueblo?"

"Yeah, of course. Where else? I don't go anywhere, not yet."

"Out here in the street?"

"No, man. Behind the hotel, there's an old furniture store, like a warehouse, empty for years. People used it to crash. Now Alex runs it. He says he owns it, but that ain't right. His bosses own it, whoever they are. The Texas guys park in there, stay there, sometimes for an hour, sometimes for a few days."

"They're smuggling women and kids?"

She nodded. "Those men scare the shit out of me."

Mat's disappearance had suddenly taken a dangerous turn. I couldn't believe he'd been involved in human trafficking, but I didn't doubt what Jeannie told me.

"But you said Mat worked with Alex?"

"He helped out." Her eyes brightened as though a switch had been turned, and suddenly she found her voice. She was eager to talk about Mat. "He wasn't around when the Texas guys were. He didn't do anything with them. At least, from what I saw. But he'd tell me that he had to get supplies for Alex, like bottled water, food, clothes. Mat was good at that kind of stuff. He knew how to get things, even without money. He told me he was helping people he'd never meet, and they'd never know anything about him. I asked for an explanation, but he wouldn't tell me more. He helped people. So he was helping those people in the back of the vans. That's why I liked him. He helped me."

"You were in one of the vans?"

"No man. I ain't no illegal. I meant he helped me with bullshit here in Pueblo. He did me a favor."

She stumbled over her last words, and I thought she was going to cry, just like Alicia and Connor had done when they talked about Mat. *What was it about Mat that had that effect on his friends?*

"You all right?"

She straightened up and nodded. She sucked in her breath and sniffled. "Yeah, no problem." No tears appeared on her face. She was harder than Alicia and Connor.

"You think something happened to him? Something bad? Could the Texans or Alex hurt him?"

She shrugged. "Not Alex. I don't know about the others. The last time I saw Mat, he said he had to hit the road fast. He took off in the middle of the night. He'd been here only like two days. I thought he was going home. I texted him, but he never answered. I figured he was through with Pueblo. Nothing here to keep him, I guess." She closed her eyes for an instant.

"Not even you?" I asked. "Was he your boyfriend?"

She laughed. "Please. Mat was a friend. A good friend, but that's all. Besides, he was hung up about some girl at his school."

"He told you about that?"

"Yeah, we talked about a lot of stuff. He knew everything. We called him Einstein, I told you that. But he was all moon-eyed about some shorty at his school. Only time I saw Mat turned out like any other asshole. She messed him up. He called her the cheerleader. Real nerdy crap. I hated her and I didn't even know her."

We sat in the shop for another half-hour. She drank two more cups of tea, finished the wrap, then ate a muffin. She talked about Pueblo and Long Beach, California, where her mother lived and where she intended to go. I'd heard similar stories before, from other wasted storytellers, but I listened closely and watched the ache play out on her face. The mother had run off when Jeannie was an infant.

"She didn't want to be a mother," Jeannie said. "She wasn't ready, not much older than I am now. I don't blame her, really. She must've had it rough. My father is an asshole, a real piece of shit."

She stopped. She wasn't going to tell me anything more about her father. She couldn't.

"Your mother kept in touch?" I asked.

"Yeah, kind of. I found her a year ago. We've been talking. She said it would be okay for me to join her in California. I'm leaving good old Pueblo as soon as I have the money."

I didn't ask why her mother didn't send her money. That's as far as she made it in the conversation. She reached her limit, and the eagerness to talk vanished. She slipped away into a cocoon that she must have made for herself when she needed a shield.

She had nothing else to tell me about Mat or Alex or the mean-looking men from Texas. I offered to give her a ride to wherever she wanted, but she turned me down and said she was going back to The Rising Sun.

She left me at the corner, and I watched the girl walk away, worn down, bruised, alone. I turned in the direction of the Sangre hotel. I had to finish up with Alex.

Twelve

Alex answered my knock with a phone in one hand and a gun in the other. He looked genuinely surprised when he saw me, and he stepped back in the room, off-balance. I rushed into the room before he could do anything to stop me.

"What the . . ." he started to say.

"I thought of a few more questions. Won't take long."

He pointed the gun at me. "You're one crazy motherfucker. Get the fuck out of my room."

The temperature in the room must've risen by ten degrees since Jeannie and I left. His sweating face wrinkled into a phony smile.

"Easy, there. You gonna shoot me? You sure you want cops around here, asking questions? I don't think you'd appreciate the attention."

"I said get out. Don't think I won't use this. I'll fucking shoot you. Guys get shot, beat-up, knifed around here all the time. You're trespassing, trying to steal something. I shoot you, makes my day. I don't care about no cops. And they don't care what happens in this shithole."

The phone in his left hand buzzed and he jerked his arm. The phone made a loud ringing noise like a train whistle. He jammed it to his ear and for a split second his attention wasn't on me. The caller must've been somebody important. I stepped into him with a hard punch to his chin. A sharp pain flashed through my knuckles, but he fell backwards. The phone flew in one direction, the gun in another. He dropped to the floor and I pounced on him. He struggled and tried to kick me, but I had him. I hit him a few more times, and he finally quit struggling. I climbed off him, picked up the gun, shut the door to his room and made him sit in one of the wobbly chairs.

"You're gonna regret this," he squeaked. "You don't know what you've got yourself into. But you're gonna learn. You're a dead man." His words were ugly and tough, but he looked worried and disoriented.

"Cheap talk from a man I just knocked down."

I had a choice. I could smash his face with the gun and hope that worked to get him to talk about Mat, or I could try to persuade him without any blood or violence. I leaned to option number one, but I reigned myself in and decided to try to talk with the guy. Not that I didn't want to hurt him. Whatever he was into, it might've resulted in Mat's disappearance, and he should have to pay for that. And I didn't like the little weasel and the way he made money. Hurting him would almost make me feel righteous. But I also believed that Alex was just enough of a survivor that pounding this guy into submission would probably take a few hours and might not result in anything useful. I didn't have much time to find Mat. Talking seemed like the more prudent, and efficient, choice.

"Do you know where Mat is?" I asked. "That's all I want. There's no need for any of this drama. I don't care what you're up to, who you work for or why you answered the door with a gun in your hand. All I care about is Mat. Give me information about him, and I'm out of your life, out of Pueblo. That's all I need."

A thin trickle of blood slipped out of the corner of his mouth. He spit on the floor and rubbed his jaw. "Yeah, you're a dead man."

I raised the gun over my head like I was going to hit him again. He flinched and defensively held up his hands. "Okay, okay. Don't hit me, you sonofabitch. I'll tell you what I know about your fucking missing cousin."

"Good. Start with the last time you saw him, a month or so ago."

He spit blood again. "Mat helped me out, that's all. Smart kid, he knew the score. He hunted down things I needed for some people I work with. Supplies for long trips. Food, water. The basics. He'd give those to me, and I'd give them to . . . uh . . . to the people I work with."

"How much was Mat involved with your smuggling?"

"Hey, guy, I didn't say anything about smuggling."

"Cut the crap and tell me what I want. Then you and I are done. I don't like this any more than you."

"Oh, we ain't done. You ain't gonna make it out of Pueblo."

I slapped him with my open palm.

"Sonofabitch!" he hollered.

"I'll make it easy for you. I'll tell you what I know, you fill in the details."

"You don't know shit."

"You and your Texas pals are working some kind of coyote trafficking scheme. The guys in the trucks and vans transport people across the border. The Texans come all the way up here to Pueblo with their cargo, so obviously there's more going on than simply getting across the border. The people being smuggled don't realize what's happening until it's too late to run."

Alex blinked like I'd hit him with another punch. I was telling him more than he thought I knew.

"They stop here, where *you* must have the information they need about where to go next. I figure the women and girls end up in sex shops or working as maids on a rich pig's estate or ranch. Maybe the men go to farms in the deep south, or they herd sheep in the Wyoming mountains. It's slavery. And you're in the thick of it."

He shook his head but didn't say anything.

"Mat did what he could to help the people in the trucks when they were in Pueblo. Food, water, basics. I doubt the Texans are the kind of gentlemen who would allow a teenager to poke into their business, so they must not know, which means you let Mat do what he did, and you didn't tell your partners what was going on. Sound right so far?"

He rotated his neck and took a couple of deep breaths. "Look, man . . . I don't smuggle people. Neither did Mat. I'm like a middleman. These people . . ."

"The Texans?"

"Yeah, *los Tejanos.* They needed a place here in Colorado, like a rest stop. From here they go east or further north. They don't do anything around here except sleep, eat and feed the cargo. I provide the place to sleep and the food. I'm the manager of the warehouse. That's all."

"What about Mat?"

"Mat understood what was going on. He did what he could to take care of the . . . uh . . . the passengers. He was that kind of kid. Smart, but kind of stupid about worrying for other people, as if they wouldn't turn on him if they had to. He was that way with some of those kids in the shelter, like that Jeannie who brought you to me. He took care of her when he was in town, but that little skank ain't worth it. I warned him, but he wouldn't listen. I let him do his thing because he was useful. If I needed something done, he'd do it, as long as no one got hurt. I thought he could get into the business full-time. But he left without telling me he was leaving, and it's not looking good for him, since *you're* trying to find him."

"You didn't have anything to do with him disappearing?"

"Why would I do that? I told you, he was helpful. I could use him around here. I wanted him to move to Pueblo, be full-time." He sat back in the chair and tilted his head backwards, to stop the bleeding in his mouth, I guessed.

"And the people you work with? Think they could've hurt him?"

"Anything's possible. Those cowboys are crazy. But there's no reason. Mat didn't cross anybody. I got no bitch with him. He just disappeared one night. If he got into trouble, it was about something that happened somewhere else. Not here in Pueblo."

I didn't completely believe Alex. He had no reason to tell me anything about Mat, and what he did tell me was said, most likely, only to stop me from hitting him. But hammering the guy wouldn't result in more information. He looked relieved when I told him I was leaving. I thought about taking his gun but decided to leave it. I wasn't worried that he'd shoot me in the Sangre Hotel, and I had no intention of ever seeing him again.

I'd learned that Mat the runaway teenager apparently did what he could for victims of human trafficking, and that he'd taken off from Pueblo in the same way he'd left Melton . . . without a word to his friends, without an explanation and without leaving any clue as to where he was going.

I sat in my pickup, again, and checked what I was doing. The traffickers from Texas might've done something to Mat. Jeannie described them as "mean," and it was not a stretch to think that if they knew about Mat and his good intentions, they would stop him. Maybe they thought he was a security risk, or a snitch. Maybe Alex put something in their heads to make Mat their target. I'd have to confront at least one of them to test that scenario, and that could only happen if I stayed in Pueblo and watched Alex until they showed up. That was something I didn't want to do.

Something that I had to do was inform the police about the warehouse behind the Sangre Hotel.

Alex said that whatever made Mat leave Pueblo had nothing to do with Pueblo. If he was right, then I had to get back to Melton and dig deeper or figure out where else he might've run to after Pueblo. Albuquerque was still in the mix. *Was that next?*

I felt tired and useless. I wasn't any closer to finding Mat, even though I knew more about him than anyone in his hometown.

I thought about driving to Denver. That meant quitting. Corrine wouldn't like it. I considered calling my sister and going over everything with her, but I wasn't up to it. Fatigue made me put Corrine on hold. *Maybe in the morning,* I thought. I decided to find a motel far from the Sangre Hotel, get some sleep and then decide whether I should head back to Denver.

Yeah, I spent one night too many in Pueblo.

Thirteen

The motel was decent enough. Clean, no noise and cheap. Nothing fancy, a basic room with a bed and toilet. The Highway 50 Rest-A-Torium was located on the northern edge of Pueblo, close to the interstate. Whatever my plan was going to be, I figured I'd get an early start. I hadn't decided the direction I would take, but I counted on choosing the right one when I had to. North to Denver, south to New Mexico? Come morning, I'd know. Somewhere in that mushy thinking was the inescapable fact that I had to do something about the trafficking racket.

Ending up in a Pueblo motel was the product of the classic Gus Corral process: seat of the pants decision-making spurred on by being in the wrong place at the wrong time. My career was marked by a makeshift method of working a case—step by uncertain step, distracted by too many details, overlooking the big picture, relying on coincidence. My clients were usually satisfied with my results. But so far, in my short time as a professional investigator, I'd been more lucky than smart, although getting knocked around by a baseball bat couldn't really be called good luck.

After I'd eaten and watched a couple of hours of rerun TV, I drifted into a restless sleep filled with dreams—more like shadowy figures whose faces I couldn't see, and all I could latch onto were anxious feelings, dread, insecurity. Mat played a role in the dreams, as well as Jeannie and Alex and Wes Delgado, but it wasn't clear what they were doing.

Around two in the morning, something woke me up. Again, more of a feeling than anything specific. I tossed the blanket off me and sat up in the bed. The door rattled. Before I fully woke and could move off the bed, the door slammed open. Two men in cowboy hats rushed into the room. One of them jumped me, smothered my mouth and pinned me down, while the other one looked outside, closed the door and turned to me with a gun in his hand. He put his finger to his lips and said, "Not a sound."

I was pinned to the mattress, unable to move. I hoped somebody heard the door bang against the wall and would do something about the noise, but it was a faint hope that quickly faded away.

The man holding me down was big and heavy. His left hand covered my mouth and his right pushed my neck into the mattress. I had trouble breathing. The man's fingers smelled like gasoline.

The man with the gun walked to the bed and pointed the gun at my head. "You hassled our friend Alex. Normally, I don't give a damn about what that punk's up to, but he let it slip that you were asking about our business. That, I do give a damn about. So, what you doing, bud? Alex said you're a snoop, looking for a missing kid? And you think Alex had something to do with it? And maybe our business? Or are you a fucking cop? Too many questions. You've made me anxious, and I need you to tell me what the hell you're doing, and what you want." He surveyed the room, slowly. "But listen," he said, "before you start talking . . . be careful with your answers. The guy holding you down gets excited easily. He could snap that neck without too much effort if you agitate him with what you say."

As if on cue, the guy on top of me squeezed my neck and pushed downward. I struggled to breathe but all I could manage was a grunt and short kicks with my trapped legs. I felt like I was passing out, when the man eased up on my neck, and I sucked in air.

I stared at the gun and tried to talk. It took some effort, but I managed. "I'm looking for my cousin's son," I said. "Mat Montoya. He ran away, came to Pueblo. That's my only reason for being here. I don't care about anything else, including whatever racket you're into. I don't even know who you are."

"Good. We'll keep it that way. This kid you're looking for? He worked with Alex, right? I told Alex to cool it with the runaways. He should've listened to me."

The guy holding me down grunted agreement.

The man in charge continued. "Alex said the kid mixed in things he shouldn't. Kind of like you. You should follow your cousin's example and disappear. Before someone helps you vanish. Got it?"

"My cousin's boy helped out, that's all I know. You'd have to ask Alex if you want more. Like I said, all I care about is Mat. But he's not around here anymore. I believe that. I'm leaving Pueblo tomorrow. Nothing here for me."

The guy with the gun tapped the shoulder of the man holding me down on the bed. The second man squeezed my neck, and again I thought I was going to pass out.

"Okay, that's enough. Let him go. I think we made our point and the snoop knows the score. He says he's leaving town. We'll be watching." He laughed. "You should get a real early start tomorrow."

He tucked the gun into the back of his jeans and walked to the door. The man holding me jumped off the bed and followed.

"Don't go looking for Alex," the first man said. "He's on vacation and got nothing to say to you. Stay out of Pueblo."

They were gone as quickly as they'd shown up. I heard a truck start up and drive away. I didn't bother to look out my window. I rubbed my neck, drank some water and laid back on the bed.

The smell of gasoline lingered in the room, and my neck felt bruised and raw. I couldn't get back to sleep, and I didn't feel like calling Corrine, or anyone else. I fell into a semiconscious trance filled with vivid images. The man who'd held me down bounced my head on the floor while he gripped my neck with iron fingers. In the background, Alex laughed and sad-eyed Jeannie danced to a slow blues song whose name I couldn't remember.

I left Pueblo the next day, at five in the morning. I drove north on I-25, towards Denver. A new pickup followed me for a few miles, but it finally turned off. That's when I pulled over and called Rob López, the chief of the Melton Police Department.

Fourteen

I talked with Chief López on the phone three different times. He was leery about what I might want, but the deeper I got into what was happening in Pueblo, the more interested he became. I wasn't sure how he'd deal with a call from me, but at least it gave him something to do. He coordinated with his friends on the Pueblo force and convinced them to believe my story, which he conveyed with urgency, or so he assured me. By the third call, I'd driven back into the outskirts of Pueblo and parked, but not near the Highway 50 Rest-A-Torium.

López said he kind of understood my reason for still looking for the boy—tying loose ends. "But you should know something," he said. "Alicia and Conner received another text message from Mat, this one saying he'd been delayed but he was still on his way home. He might make it back before you get out of Pueblo."

"That'd be great," I said. "Anyone actually talk with Mat?"

"Not yet."

He also said that a cop in Lubbock, Texas called to say that a kid matching Mat's description had been seen hitchhiking on the edge of town, but he was long gone.

"Again, good news, in a way," I said.

I was on a residential street that led to an indoor mall when I talked to López for the final time that day. From there I drove to the mall and parked, again, and waited, again. I left my truck for a hot dog from the mall's food court, then I waited some more. An hour and a half later, as I burped mustard and relish, a man and a woman in a dark blue Subaru Outlander pulled up beside my truck. The man, dressed in jeans and a blue polo shirt, joined me in the cab of my truck. The woman waited behind the Subaru's steering wheel.

"I'm Detective Grossman," the man said. He flashed a badge. "You know what's happening, right?"

He was young for a detective. A full head of brown hair framed a tan face, and brown eyes squinted at me as though he wore uncomfortable contact lenses.

"I know what López told me," I said.

"Good. I just finished going over everything with Rob. He's a good man, got a lot of friends in Pueblo, especially on the job. None of us liked it when he had to leave Pueblo. Politics, you know?"

"Uh, yeah, I guess so. He's doing okay in Melton. Far as I can tell."

"He'll do all right, no doubt. Anyway, he said you were reliable. That's enough for me. You ready?"

"The way I understand it, I'm not doing much except identifying the jerks who hassled me in my motel room, if you find them."

He nodded.

"I should be able to handle that."

"We're set," he said. "Everyone's in place, waiting on me to take you to the warehouse. We should go."

"You guys move fast. I only talked with López today."

"We've been trying to seal the deal on these guys for a while now. Rob vouched for you, stressed that you will identify the men who threatened and assaulted you. And that you'll testify when we need you. It's the piece we need. That's enough for a warrant to raid the warehouse. You're the best link we have that connects what we know is going on with specific people. With a little luck, we'll catch them with a van filled with women." He looked around the parking lot. "We appreciate what you're doing. Takes a certain kind of guts to stick your neck out like you're doing."

"Or a certain kind of stupidity," I said.

I didn't know what to do with gratitude from a cop. Two or three of my Denver friends would never talk to me again if they learned that I'd snitched to the cops. But I had no regrets. My throat still ached from the manhandling by my unwelcome midnight visitors. And there was a very real probability that they had done something bad to Mat. The arrest of the two cowboy thugs might finally provide some answers for George and Essie.

Detective Grossman signaled his partner, then directed me to follow Detective Rivera. Twenty minutes later, I was parked almost in the same spot I'd used when I checked out The Rising Sun shelter. The detective told me to sit tight in my truck. He and Rivera sprinted to the Sangre Hotel, where, I assumed, they would meet up with the rest of their team. I liked the fact that I'd put into motion an action that might make a difference, do some good. Corrine would be proud.

Fifteen minutes later, the streets echoed with gunshots, explosions and the heavy clang of metal banging metal. Sirens wailed in the distance. The homeless people on the corner bolted in a half-dozen different directions. They pushed their loaded grocery carts, some hollering and cussing, others in a quiet frenzy as they rushed to escape the noise and danger. A trio of teenagers emerged from the shelter, saw the scrambling homeless people, then jumped back inside.

Several minutes passed. They were filled with more noise—gunshots, sirens. Then, total quiet, and I realized I was the only person on the street. I was tempted to leave my truck and head to the warehouse. I had to do something. I just wasn't sure what.

Jeannie appeared from around the corner before I made my move. The cowboy who'd held a gun to my head followed her, close, too close. He gripped her elbow and jammed a pistol in her ribs. Tear streaks lined her cheeks, and all color had drained from her face. The man violently shoved her to The Rising Sun's door. He pushed Jeannie into the entranceway, looked over his shoulder, then ducked in.

I waited for a Pueblo cop to come running around the corner, in hot pursuit. No one appeared. The knot in my gut tightened. I imagined the girl and the other kids in the shelter, at the mercy of a man who kidnapped and sold women. I guessed that Toni Marriot was no match.

I grabbed a crowbar from behind the truck's seat and jumped out. I ran to the sidewalk, rounded the corner and circled the shelter. I counted on finding an open back entrance. The narrow alley was littered with trash and dog shit. Smoke and the acrid smell of gunfire from the warehouse lingered over the alley. A Rising Sun sign hung loosely on a door near an overflowing dumpster. I eased the door open and entered a dark foyer separated from the rest of the building by a torn curtain.

The cowboy's voice boomed through the hallways. "Keep your heads on the goddamn floor! I'll shoot the first one who says anything. Stay down! Nobody moves!"

I peeked through the curtain. The four teenagers and Marriot were stretched out on their stomachs, their hands behind their heads. The cowboy focused on the front door, his back to me. Every few seconds he'd glance over his shoulder at the curtain. I thought about what I should do and what the risks were. The odds weren't good. My hands shook and the crowbar felt hot and heavy. I thought of the terrible things that were going to happen—to the girls on the floor or to me—whether I acted or not.

I waited until the man's attention was again on the front door, then I ran through the curtain and smashed the tire iron into the cowboy's back. His knees buckled. He grunted and arched forward. I raised the crowbar above my head, but he whirled and crashed into my legs. I fell to the stained floor. He aimed his gun at me, and I rolled to my side. The gunshot echoed in my ears. Someone screamed. Pieces of the hardwood floor bounced off my ears. Jeannie jumped up from the floor, leaped at the cowboy and hugged his legs. He flailed his arms like a mad ape, trying to wrench the girl off his body. She hung on with all she had, but she couldn't keep her grip. The man bellowed, kicked his legs and slammed his gun into Jeannie's ribs. She crumbled back to the floor. The man raised his gun again. I swung the tire iron into his hand, and the gun flew across the room. He shouted something I couldn't understand. That's when Toni Marriot smashed the back of his head with the coffeepot. Blood squirted from the man's scalp and he pitched to his side. I stood over him, expecting him to do something, but he was out.

Fifteen

I spent the next several hours with Detectives Grossman and Rivera. I gave them the entire backstory of how I ended up in Pueblo, my interaction with Jeannie and Alex, my motel confrontation with the cowboy goons and my connection to Rob López. When I finished telling them the story, the detectives had me write it all down. I also officially identified the unconscious cowboy and his wounded pal as the two men who had assaulted and threatened me in the motel. Grossman told me their names were Randolph Scuggins and Macario Torres, which meant nothing to me but was enough for the detectives to high five each other and grin like clowns on Ecstasy.

I didn't see Jeannie. Grossman explained that she was looking for Alex when Scuggins grabbed her as he ran from the warehouse. They ended up in the Center because the girl told him she could get a car from the Center's Director, "which was a brilliant lie," according to the detective. Grossman explained that they'd been unable to contact her father and that Pueblo County Social Services had placed the girl in a protective foster home situation. He assured me that she would be taken care of, and safe.

The raid was only partially successful. In addition to Scuggins and Macario, Grossman and Rivera arrested a trio of gunmen who surrendered when the first shots were fired. No victims were found in the warehouse, but the beaten and bullet-ridden body of Alex Temerio turned up in a back room. Grossman was confident that Scuggins and Torres were the killers and that sooner or later one of them would turn on the others involved in the trafficking ring, especially because of the threat of a conviction for Alex's murder.

"It's not all wrapped up," Grossman said. "But we've stopped it. At least we've stopped this part, for now. And all the scumbags we've arrested will get hard time. I've no doubt about that."

///

By the time I finally finished with the cops, I couldn't tell if I was exhausted or hyped up from the day's events. I was wide awake and tired, antsy *and* lethargic. I hoped Grossman was right about stopping the trafficking, but we knew the raid was a temporary set-back for whoever organized and set up the smuggling. And no women had been rescued.

On the other hand, Jeannie was safe and, I assumed, well-fed and asleep in a good bed. She'd fought to save herself, a good sign.

I talked with Grossman about Mat, and during the long night in the police building he told me that Scuggins had admitted that he knew who Mat was, but that he hadn't seen him for several weeks. The detective promised to continue to ask about Mat. I wasn't sure what I wanted: for Scuggins and Torres to admit they'd killed Mat, or for Grossman to verify that they had nothing to do with his disappearance. Neither result was satisfactory.

I left the detectives with handshakes and more cop gratitude. They were upset because agents from the FBI had swooped into town as soon as the raid was over. The case against the interstate trafficking ring would be taken out of the hands of the Pueblo police, but Grossman and Rivera could keep jurisdiction over the murder of Alex.

"It's a consolation prize, but we'll take it," Grossman said.

I needed to get out into the night air and away from the industrial green walls, bulky men and women in military-style uniforms carrying ugly weapons, and the uneasy, queasy feeling that someone was watching me and would pounce at my first misstep. Old habits die hard. Other than when I'd been arrested in the past, I hadn't spent much time in a police building, rubbing shoulders with too many cops.

I tried to talk myself into another night in a motel. I kidded myself that I could get a night's rest just about anywhere in Pueblo. *After all, the goons and thugs were locked up, right?*

I took an elevator to the first floor of the police building. When the elevator stopped on the second floor and the door opened, Toni Marriott walked in and smiled at me.

"They finally finished with you, too, huh?" she asked. "God, what a day, right? You okay? I'm beat. Worn out. Can't wait to get home, have a drink and a bath, and get to bed. You sure you're okay? I know I'm not. What a fucking day, right?" She was frenetic and intense, still wound up from the afternoon's events.

"Yeah, I'm okay. Tired. Like you."

"For sure, right?" She laughed, laughed again. The laughter stopped, and she looked at me like a mouse who bumped into the house cat. She tried to speak, but she could only manage a few sobs. Before I realized what was happening, she started to shake, and then she cried.

She fell against me and I held her up. She hugged me and continued to cry. I couldn't think of anything to say. Hell, I was in worse shape than her. But I kept it together, didn't cry much. When the elevator stopped, I helped her out of the building and to her car.

"Thank you," she said before she opened her car door. "I'm sorry I did that. I was afraid for the girls. Scared shitless, if you want the truth. Jeannie's been through so much. And now this mess. I guess it's catching up to me."

"Nothing to be sorry about," I said. "I was as afraid as anybody in that room. You are absolutely right that this has been a long day. I'm wiped out."

She climbed in her car, turned it on and lowered the window. "You need a place to stay, don't you?"

"I was thinking that I'd drive to Denver tonight. I won't sleep anyway."

"Oh, hell no. You can't do that. What if something happens to you on the way? I couldn't take it. I feel guilty enough about what happened to Jeannie and the other kids. I can't be responsible for you too."

"Then I'll find a room somewhere. I'll manage." She grabbed my hand through the open window. "And you're not responsible for me."

She let go of my hand and tapped her steering wheel a few times. She looked up at me. "I got an extra blanket and pillow. You can sleep on the couch. It's the least I can do after what you did today. I'd offer the bed, but I don't have a clean set of sheets, so a billet on the couch is the best I can do."

"You don't have to do that."

"I know I don't have to. I want to. It's just a place to sleep. Anyways, if Jeannie hears that I sent you on your way without helping you, she'd never let me forget it. That girl can be a supreme bitch." She smiled at her words.

I was too tired to argue. And anything other than a motel room sounded great. "Okay. I'll follow you."

The twenty-minute drive to Toni Marriot's small house in Pueblo West happened without me noticing any details. I really was worn out. All I remember about the drive were the bouncing red balls from the taillights on her car that guided me through Pueblo's dark streets and up to the curb in front of her house, where I somehow managed to park.

I looked up and down the street, then slowly climbed out of the truck. I locked the doors and listened. I heard only the familiar sounds of a sleeping city.

She greeted me at her front door with an open can of beer. "Thought you might need this," she said.

I sat down on a soft couch, settled back on pillows and embroidered furniture coverings, and stretched my legs. She disappeared. Music came on from somewhere—Dwight Yoakum singing broken-hearted-cowboy songs. She reappeared with her own beer and eased herself onto the couch next to me.

I told her the same story I'd told the detectives, including my run-in with the ghost of Running Elk. She laughed at that and apologized for acting like a jerk, as she put it, when I first stopped at The Rising Sun.

"No worries," I said. "I get why you do that."

She appeared genuinely interested in my search for Mat and asked if there was anything she could do to help.

"He's a good kid, smart as hell," she said. "He helped me around the Center. That's how he is. Helpful. I like Mat. But, you know, he could be anywhere. The last time he was here in Pueblo, he stayed for only a few days, a weekend. He left in a hurry. Said he had places to be, people to see. I assumed he was going home, but who knows? These kids move around like angels in the wind. They surprise me with what they'll do. They're not afraid of the craziest shit, but then, the smallest thing can throw them, and they're lost. We do what we can for them, but I've seen so many come through the Center. Then they leave, and I never see them again." She sighed. "I hope he's okay."

She was less uptight than when she was at the police station, but every so often she'd nervously tap her foot and have to stand up. We continued to talk about Mat, runaways, the financial crisis she faced every month at the Center. She gave me her history: born in Chicago, earned degrees from the university in Boulder, landed in Pueblo when she had to escape a "sticky domestic situation" in Boulder, and then she described how much she loved her work and the quirky city of Pueblo. I said a few things about Denver, and my sisters and the dead end town of Melton, but for the most part I let her dominate the conversation. She needed to expel a few demons, and talking seemed a good way to do that. I wasn't much of a conversationalist on my best days, let alone after one when I had to deal with a crazed cowboy and his gun. She brought out a bottle of Johnny Walker, we had a couple of shots and we both finally relaxed.

"I don't do drugs, so I can't offer you anything," she said.

"No problem," I said.

"The drug conversation never ends at the Center. That and my tirades about vaping. I don't want the kids to think I'm a hypocrite, so for me it's an occasional drink in the privacy of my home."

"Johnny Walker is fine."

I can't say that I was surprised when she invited me to her bed. That wasn't my intention when I followed her to her house, and I didn't think of myself as the guy who ends up in bed with the lonely stranger. I was just another slightly whacked out Northside Denver dude trying to get his bearings. But it happened. Neither one of us was embarrassed or overwhelmed. It just happened, and the two of us made everything all right, at least for that night.

Sixteen

The one-night stand turned into one more day and night in Pueblo. That day wasn't anything like the memories I had of my youthful trips to the Steel City, but the final effect was the same. The summer sun revived my sore bones and aching muscles, and Toni's cool touch took care of my lingering head-tripping and tendency to wander to the dark side. We managed to repair some of the mental damage caused by the wild man in The Rising Sun, although the events around the raid were never far from our awareness. We talked out what we could and ignored the rest.

She turned the Center over to one of her volunteers—nobody could fault her for taking time off. We walked along the Riverwalk and watched the copper-tinged sunset from her small and weedy backyard.

I called everyone I thought should hear from me. That meant long conversations with George Montoya, Essie Montoya, Rob López and my sister Corrine.

George and Essie were surprised that I was still looking for Mat, given the text messages. I used the same reasoning I'd tried on López: I liked to have everything wrapped up before I closed a case, and until Mat showed up, I thought I should talk with anyone who might have information about him. I told George I was working on my own dime, just in case he thought I was wasting his money. He didn't seem to mind.

"As long as Mat shows up, you can talk to anyone you want, go anywhere you want. It's all good."

I gave each of them the details and outcome of my Pueblo visit, almost word for word. Essie and George were shocked that Mat was involved with traffickers and a man who'd been murdered.

They didn't dwell on it, though. The text messages were all they needed to reassure themselves.

When they asked me what I was going to do next, my stock answer was that I needed to think that out, although it looked like I should go back to the beginning: Melton. I had more loose ends that needed to be tied up so that I could try to make sense of everything that had happened, and so that I would be prepared if things didn't work out the way we hoped.

López agreed. "You should swing back through here. Wes Delgado is going to be released from the hospital in another day or so," he said. "I'm going to wait at the hospital door for him, and then he goes back to jail. I want to know more about that missing backpack, and what he knew about Mat's involvement with the traffickers. It won't surprise me if Scuggins knows more about Mat than he's letting on, and Delgado might know more about *that,* if he really was a friend of Mat's."

"Those are the things I want to talk to him about, too," I said.

"I thought so. You can ask him whatever you want when he's twiddling his thumbs in the jail."

I agreed, and we planned to meet the next day, assuming Delgado had been released from the hospital.

George and Essie also wanted me to return. They wanted to hear more details about Mat's history in Pueblo, even though I assured them I'd told them everything I knew.

I finished rehashing the recent events with a call to Corrine. She also assumed that the answer to Mat's disappearance could very well rest with Scuggins and the traffickers.

"And that's a problem," she said. "The breakup of the operation will piss off some people. You *have* pissed off some people. You should come home, at least for a few days. Let things cool down. I'm worried about you. I didn't think your looking for George's boy would turn into such a mess. But that's you, ain't it? Trouble follows you like our old dog, Chato, used to tag along after Dad. At least here in Denver you have friends and family. I can watch your back."

Good old Corrine, ready to defend me at the same time that she wanted to slap me silly like she did when we were kids and I had screwed up, again.

"I appreciate the offer, but I'll be home before you know it. If anyone comes after me in Melton, the entire county will know it before they park their fancy pickups. No one enters that town without being watched and then talked about. I'll know if anyone's coming. And I'll be careful."

"You were in bad shape when you left. You worse now? And be honest."

"You won't believe this, but I feel better. I still have headaches and once in a while I slip into a mood, you know. But right now, today, I'm okay, and that's what matters."

"Must be that woman. I repeat: Be careful, Gus." I felt more than heard her sigh. "Does it do me any good to tell you that?"

"Don't worry. That's all I can say."

"Oh hell, brother. That's what I do. But I get it. You have to keep constant pressure on the wheel. That's who you are. And this is *familia*."

"Right. You always say family comes first."

Then I returned my attention to Toni.

She decided she could talk to me about Mat. She liked the boy, that was apparent. In her view, Mat could do no wrong. She went on and on about how much he worked around the Center and how he helped the younger kids.

"The perfect role model," she said. "Not the typical boy who passes through The Rising Sun."

I reminded her that he was a chronic runaway, and that he had caused a good amount of pain to his family and friends in his hometown.

"I don't doubt that," she said. "He didn't strike me as the kind of kid who hates his family or that he was trying to get away from a home situation he couldn't handle. But I didn't understand everything that was going on with him. He couldn't give a good reason for his running away, and I didn't push him for an explanation. There's always something, though, and it's usually serious. The kids who come to the Center aren't just acting out for a weekend or trying to scare their parents into buying something they want, like a car or a phone. The kids tell me the serious stuff when they're ready. But sometimes they never do. That was Mat."

"He didn't let on what was driving him?"

"Not really." She thought for a second. "He had that thing about his girlfriend. That messed him up, big time. That's what he said. But I never got the impression that the breakup was so bad that he had to hit the road. Now that I think about it, he never wanted to talk about it for long. He did bring it up one day, and when I tried to find out more, he brushed it aside. I think he was embarrassed that he'd even mentioned it. You know how teenaged boys can be about girls. Especially girlfriends who dump them."

"He couldn't get over her?"

"Yeah, something happened when they broke up, I guess. That was my impression. You know, he said more than once that he had to bring closure to that situation. That's why I thought he was going back to Melton when he left here the last time."

"I've met the girl and her parents. That was unreal . . . surreal. Did he say anything about Doctor Cleary and his wife?"

"Not that I remember. He didn't dwell on it, and he closed me off when I brought it up a few times. If there was something going on between Mat and the parents, he kept it to himself."

"The good people of Melton think they know Mat, but they're wrong. They have no idea about what he was doing in Pueblo. You say he kept stuff to himself. He was closed off in his hometown, too. As near as I can tell, everyone liked the kid but he had only one real friend, a kid named Conner, and maybe a weirdo who calls himself Wes Delgado."

She shook her head. "He told me about Conner and Delgado. Mat liked Conner, but said he was too needy sometimes, too much of a lapdog—that's what he called him. And Delgado . . . no way. Mat didn't trust him, called him a con man. I don't think Mat was his friend. In fact, Mat said he had info on the guy that the cops in Melton would want to know. He said he wouldn't snitch, but he didn't sound sure about himself."

"Yeah, Delgado never fit in with Mat, and Conner did seem to be into hero worship. I've got to figure out the connections if I want to learn more about my runaway cousin."

We ran out of things to say about Mat.

"Did you know the guy that was killed? Alex? Jeannie introduced me to him."

"I heard of him. From Jeannie and some of the other kids. He dropped by the Center a couple of times, but he never talked to me. I warned her to stay away from him, but that was useless on my part. Everyone around here knew something was going on with him and that empty warehouse. I never knew what exactly."

"The cops didn't talk to you about that?"

"A while back, yeah." She hesitated. "I told them the rumors and gossip, but I didn't have anything concrete. And Jeannie and her friends never confided in me about what went on in that warehouse. That woman detective, Rivera, gave me her card and asked me to call her if I saw or heard anything specific. That was as far as it went. I should have pressed Jeannie to tell me what she knew. Maybe we could've avoided what happened. I almost got her killed because I didn't do more."

"Don't put that on yourself. The craziness didn't come from you or Jeannie or the cops. Even if you had known more that you could tell the police, chances are it would have gone down just like it did, no matter what. The raid, and then Scuggins' attempt to use Jeannie and you and the others as hostages or shields or something just as dangerous would have still played out. Scuggins and his crew are violent killers. You did what you could, and at the end, you saved everyone when you knocked him out."

I think she reluctantly accepted what I said, but she didn't completely let go of her guilt, which must've been based in part on the lingering fear she felt for the runaways. Kids at risk. Angels in the wind.

During our time together, we opened up to one another in a way that I hadn't been able to do for a long time. She described in general terms the abuse her fiancé inflicted on her when she lived in Boulder, and the intricate scheme she had to pull off to escape. She had him arrested one night when he showed up drunk and belligerent. That was the last time she'd seen him. She left her apartment before he bailed out of jail and did what she could to make him think she'd run off to Phoenix, where her sister lived. That was two years ago, and so far, her ex hadn't shown up. She worried that her very public position as director of The Rising Sun would lead him to her, but she believed she could handle it.

"I'm more aware now, and not afraid of him," she said. "I'll have him locked up if he shows his ugly face in Pueblo." She smiled at me. "Or I'll take care of him myself."

I believed her.

I reciprocated with my own stories of life as a private eye, most of which had her laughing or feeling sorry for me. For both of us, we managed to release a few things that had weighed us down. But that kind of talk can go on for only so long. We moved past our personal history of traumas and focused on where we were in the present.

When it became obvious that I should push on from Pueblo, we parted with the understanding that we would see each other again at the trial of Scuggins and Macario, if not sooner. She gave me a long and sweet goodbye kiss. On the interstate on the way out of Pueblo, I tried to preserve the image of her face and the taste of her lips.

Seventeen

The Pueblo heat followed me to Melton. A curtain-like shower pelted my pickup, but the rain didn't cool the air. Steam vapors danced on the asphalt, and inside the truck's cab the steady beat of the storm drummed into my overworked brain that the answer to Mat's disappearance had always been in the small forgotten town on the windswept Colorado prairie. I drove straight to the answer, convinced that the truth was close.

I should've felt relieved and at ease with the idea that I would soon be able to explain the mystery of Mat Montoya. But I didn't expect to be a messenger of good news. The realization of what I was thinking, and an understanding of what I had concluded about the fate of the runaway boy, choked me, made my throat tighten. I easily imagined Mat next to me in the pickup. He appeared patient, calm. He waited for me to finish my wandering.

Once again, I drove into Melton, and once again I felt like I was the only human being in the town. The few signs of life included a pair of muddy pickups parked behind the Sand Creek Saloon and a large black dog asleep in the shade of the bar's dumpster. I drove past the bar just as the rear door opened and Werm walked out, shielding his eyes from the fading sun. He lit a cigarette and leaned against the chipped brick wall. His eyes never left me as I drove past. *That's right*, I thought. *I'm still not from around here.*

I parked at the police station and waited a few minutes. I left my pickup when I believed I knew what to say to López and what to ask Delgado.

The heat smothered the town and crept into the haggard building. López greeted me with a sweaty handshake. We talked about the Pueblo raid. He wanted to know details, and I obliged. I also passed on greetings from Detective Grossman, and that resulted in a story from López about his early days on the Pueblo police force when he and Grossman worked together. I asked why he had left Pueblo, but he ignored my question and continued with his rookie cop story. When he finished, I reminded him that I was back in Melton to speak with Wes Delgado.

"Of course, of course," he said. He motioned for me to follow him to the cell.

Wes Delgado's topknot was gone. His head had been shaved. A harsh orange-brown spot stained the bandages that wrapped around his grapefruit pink neck. He looked to be in pain, and he sat on his jail cot with his head in his hands as though he wanted to rip open his face and toss away his eyes. It didn't make him any happier when he glanced up and saw Chief López and me coming towards him.

The Chief unlocked the cell, opened the heavy door and left when he locked me in with Delgado.

Delgado sweated in his cell, and in a few minutes I felt my own sweat slipping down my back.

"López put you back in here, where you hurt yourself?"

Delgado grunted.

"He trusts you not to do it again?"

He looked at me with rheumy eyes and a smirk loaded with irony. "I don't think he gives a fuck, one way or the other. What the hell you want?"

"I want all of it. The complete Mat Montoya story. All you didn't tell me when I asked the first time. What was in that backpack, why Mat left it with you and what happened to it. That's what I want."

"You are one crazy Mexican," he said. "Or plain stupid. What makes you think I know any of what you asked and, most important, why in the good goddamn would I tell you anything? The kid's coming home, in case you hadn't heard. Your job is finished, Corral, no thanks to you. Detective? My ass. Get the fuck out of my cell."

"I'm not going anywhere. You're gonna talk to me, one way or another. And López told me to stay as long as I want. You're right about one thing: he really doesn't care for you."

Delgado tried to stand up, but I pushed his elbow and he wobbled backwards to the cot.

"Take it easy," I said. "Or you will get hurt again. I know what you're feeling. I've had my neck bashed, too. Not a good place to be. But I'll smack you if you don't start talking."

I wasn't going to hit him, but my bluff might make him talk.

He held up his hands. "I think I'm going to be sick."

"No, you're not. Take a few deep breaths. Drink some water. Then you can start with the backpack. How'd you end up with it? And don't give me your bullshit. Mat didn't give it to you to keep for him. You weren't that kind of friend."

"The fuck you know? I was a better friend than his so-called pal Conner. That much I do know." I flicked my fingers on his bandage and he jerked backwards.

"Don't. I will get sick, you keep that up."

"Then start talking or you can spend the night with your vomit on the floor."

He collapsed into even more of a defeated, wasted man barely hanging on to whatever slim thread of humanity he still possessed. He didn't look like he was going to say anything.

"Why'd you do it?" I asked.

He raised his head. "What? Why did I do what? I haven't done anything to anybody. Including your lost boy. I know what you're thinking, but I didn't do nothing to that kid."

"Maybe. Yet to be seen. But I'm asking why you tried to kill yourself. It couldn't have been because López arrested you for concealing evidence. That wasn't that big of a deal."

"That's none of your fucking business." He paused, took a deep breath and let out a soft sigh. "I'm tired, that's all. Tired of the bullshit and the dead ends and the wasted time. You feel me? Tired, man. That's all."

"You don't get any sympathy from me. We all have to live, or die, with our choices. You made some dumb ones. I'm sorry, but that's the way it is."

"Fuck you. Go back to Denver. Leave me alone."

"You know that ain't gonna happen, Wes. Before I leave, you're going to talk to me. You might as well get started, before I bounce your head on this cot. How do you think that will feel? Think it will improve your lame-ass, take-pity-on-poor-me mood?"

"You really are a prick."

"Right, and I'm losing my patience."

I moved my shoulders as though I was about to do something physical. He flinched.

"Okay, okay," he whispered. "What the hell? All right. Mat was on his way out of town, again. He'd just returned from Pueblo, hadn't even been home. He was in a big hurry to get back on the road. He stopped by because, well, because I owed him money and he wanted it. I gave him what I had, only about fifty bucks. He was leaving my trailer when he got a call. I don't know from who, but it shook him up. He got jumpy, nervous, said he had to take care of something, but he didn't want to carry the backpack. Said he couldn't deal with it, whatever that meant. So, he left it."

"Your first story, about Mat leaving a note. You made it up?"

"It didn't happen that way. No note."

"But Mat did give you the backpack, to hold for him?"

"Right. He said for me to take it to his father, if he didn't come back for it that night."

"Mat didn't come back, but you didn't take it to George. You kept it, looked through it. And then somebody stole it from you. Is that it?"

He slumped deeper into the cot. "Yeah, that's it. Except I didn't look through it. I swear. I was going to, how could I not? But I put it away and never got to it. And when you came by the other day, I decided it was a good time to get it to George, but it was gone. That's the truth. That's all I know about that damn backpack."

"Your truth keeps changing. Who was he going to see? Who called him?"

"I told you . . . I don't know. If I knew, I'd say it. I got no reason to keep that to myself. I swear. I've told you everything."

"Let me get this right. Mat had been in Pueblo. He returned after a few days, but before he saw anyone else, he went to your place to get money. He gets a phone call, leaves in a hurry and stashes the backpack with you. But he doesn't come back for the backpack? Is that what happened?"

"Yes, that's what I remember. I figured he ran off again and that sooner or later he'd come back. It didn't turn out that way. Now leave me alone. I don't feel right."

"When Mat dropped off the backpack, how long had he been gone? You said he'd returned from Pueblo."

"Yeah, that's what he told me. He'd been there a few days, like a weekend. Then he came back, but he was leaving again. He needed money, but he took off again without the pack, and here we all are, waiting for him to return."

"As far as you know, he didn't contact George or Essie before he left again?"

"Hell, I don't know. The kid was in a big hurry. He was here, then he was gone. Now I hear he's coming back. So why in the fuck are you asking me all these questions? Ask the kid himself, when he finally shows up. And have him explain the goddamn backpack. Leave me alone. You have really screwed me up."

He lay back on the cot and covered his eyes with his arms. His pale skin looked even whiter, almost transparent.

"I'll tell López to call Cleary, the doctor. You look like shit."

I'd given myself a headache too. The timeline Delgado described didn't gibe with the way I understood Mat's disappearance, but why would Delgado make up such a scenario? The way he described events didn't free him from my suspicions. If anything, it made him look more like a suspect, because he admitted he was one of the last people to see Mat before he vanished, and he'd kept that information to himself, along with the backpack.

He'd given me all he was going to, and I didn't think pushing him any further would do either of us any good. I left him on his cot, his arms still across his face, his skin chalky and sickly.

I repeated Delgado's story to López and suggested he call the doctor to look at his prisoner. He said he would, and then he asked me why I was still looking for Mat.

"It's more than tying up loose ends," he said.

I nodded. "I don't believe that the text messages are from Mat. You want to know the truth . . . I think Mat's not coming home. I'm looking for Mat, yeah, but that means I'm looking for the reality of what happened to him, that's all. I owe that to George and Essie. If Mat does show up, and I hope he does, then all I've done is wasted my time. No harm, no foul. Except, apparently, to Delgado, who got sick from my questions."

López shrugged, muttered something about it was a free country and I could investigate whatever I wanted . . . as long as I didn't get in his way. Then he called Doctor Cleary, and I left.

My head throbbed with Delgado's story, and on my way to Essie's house I tried to fill in the missing pieces, but it was too much. In the midst of hazy assumptions, cloudy attempts at organizing my thoughts and half-remembered bits of conversations with Jeannie, Toni, Delgado and Essie, one thing jumped out. Someone called Mat right before he disappeared. Who was that person, and what was the message that upset Mat and made him rush to meet the caller?

Eighteen

That night at Essie's started out like the previous time I'd spent in her house. She made dinner, Felisa watched TV, I did the dishes. Then Felisa joined Essie and me in the kitchen. The two women were still excited about the prospect of Mat's return, and they talked all evening about their memories of Mat as a toddler, then a boy and now a young man.

Essie played a flash drive of music by Lila Downs, Rodrigo y Gabriela and Ray Charles. I listened to the animated women talk about the boy they adored and missed, and every few minutes a bluesy, exotic melody from the background grabbed my attention. I kept struggling to keep my sadness at bay, and forced myself to listen to the women and not the music.

Felisa was especially sentimental, and her eyes teared up more than once. But she needed to talk about her grandson. The talk wound up both women, and Felisa surprised me with her energy. Although Essie tried to end the conversation several times, Felisa kept on, even as she yawned and her eyelids drooped. When the old woman finally went to bed, Essie and I sat in the kitchen, where we continued our emotional talk and shared a bottle of wine. The heady night continued with more stories, laughter and tears.

I retold the summary of what had happened in Pueblo and what I'd learned. She had a difficult time believing that Mat was in any way connected to smugglers and traffickers, but she came around when I explained that his role seemed to be only to help the victims. That was the Mat she knew and loved.

She also had a hard time believing Delgado's story. Mat would have made his presence known if he had returned to Melton from Pueblo, she insisted. "And for sure he wouldn't have left again without saying something to George, or me, even Alicia or Connor," she said. "He knows we worry about him. I can't believe it. He stopped by Delgado's place and didn't have time to check in with his family? No, I don't buy it."

"He was in a hurry about something. Any ideas about that?" I poured wine in my glass and offered her the bottle.

"Go ahead. It's all yours."

I topped my glass with the last of the wine.

"No thoughts about the phone call that Delgado says shook Mat up?" I asked.

"Could be anything, if Delgado is telling the truth, which I doubt." She sipped her wine. "Look, Gus. I appreciate all you've done. I never would've thought that Mat could be associated with anyone like the gang you ran into in Pueblo. I'll talk to Mat about that, make sure he stays away from those people, and I'll try to get to the bottom of why he feels the need to run away. Now that he's coming home, we can clear up all these questions you have with him directly, right? There won't be any more mystery about where he's been or who he was with, or backpacks or phone calls, or anything like that. Mat will have all the answers. Right?"

"Yeah, you're right. Just my obsessive personality. I'm sorry to be such a buzzkill. I'll stop. Mat will clear up everything."

She smiled, with a little too much condescension, I thought. But I let it go. She was family, and she wanted to think only good thoughts about the happy return of her nephew and the positive resolution of the puzzle of where he spent his time. I couldn't hold that against her.

She looked at the wall clock. "Wow, it got late. You're good company, Gus. Time flies."

It was almost midnight. "I'm gonna call it a day," I said. "Too much driving today."

She stood up, hesitated, then sat back down. The wine hit Essie hard. Her smile broadened into a bright ribbon of teeth spread across the front of her face. A pink flush bordered her eyes and nose. She wobbled to her feet again and whispered. The way she spoke made it sound like we were involved in a late night, dark-web conspiracy.

"If you're willing to go for another drive, I think I can solve one of your mysteries. . . . With a little luck, and good timing. I think you'll like it." She giggled.

"Now you're being too mysterious yourself. What's up?"

Her words flowed quickly, if not clearly. "Let's go find Running Elk, the ghost that almost ran you off the road. You up for that?"

I didn't think too hard about what she asked. "Lead the way," I said, not sure what I was agreeing to.

"To Old Smokey," she said.

She giggled as she locked her house and again during the short walk to my truck. Off to the northeast, lightning opened the sky. A few seconds later, thunder rolled over us and a quick gust of fecund air cooled my skin, washing away the remaining heat of Pueblo. I felt a shift in the atmosphere.

"Good night to see a ghost," I said when we were on the way.

I wasn't serious, but she only giggled. I humored her, played along with the joke. I assumed Essie simply needed to go for a ride, to get some air, let off a little steam. Relax. I needed all that, too. So there I was in my shaky pickup, cruising the stormy darkness of eastern Colorado with a tearful cousin who'd had one glass too many. We were supposedly on a mission to find an old legend that no one believed.

She pointed in the direction she wanted to go, and it wasn't long before she had me turn at the sign for Gilroy Road. I recognized the hill I turned onto as the same one where I'd had my encounter with the "ghost" and almost lost control of my truck.

"Pull over, there, by that boulder and the dead cactus."

I followed her instructions.

"Cool the lights, park it. It shouldn't be much longer." The giggle was gone but I could hear the smile in her words.

"What are we waiting for?" I asked.

"Patience, cuz. Keep your eyes on the road."

Lightning lit up the sky again, closer than before. The boom of the thunder followed quickly, and I would've sworn that the pick-up rocked with the crash. Heavy drops of rain spattered the windshield and tapped the roof. Except for the seconds when lightning flashed, we were surrounded by the total blackness of the night. It wasn't hard to imagine that we were trapped in the truck, at the mercy of the storm. The rain sped up and water rushed around the truck as though a vein in the earth's crust had opened, and a dozen streams of black blood erupted in the dry hard dirt of the prairie.

I was about to turn on the wipers when Essie sat upright and pointed out my window. I turned to my left and I saw it. A dark shape weaved along the road, hunched over in the rain. At first, I thought the figure wore a headdress of some sort. As it came closer, I could make out a man's head covered with a hooded windbreaker. Rain glistened on the smooth jacket, and his arms pumped at his side, keeping pace with his feet. He moved straight ahead, and I was sure he didn't see us, although we were only about ten yards from him. The hooded figure jogged into the night, and the rain and darkness swallowed him.

"What is George doing?" I whispered to Essie. "What's going on?"

"He runs when he can't sleep, which is almost every night, usually at this time, midnight; sometimes later, sometimes earlier. He told me he comes out here to clear his head, to forget. He blocks out everything except the ground and rocks and the cactus and sage. He has to or he'll fall and hurt himself in the dark. He has to focus, or he'll go over a cliff, get lost, trip into an arroyo."

"In the dark? How can he do that? I can barely make it down these roads in my truck, and that's with headlights."

"George grew up out here. He camped around here as a kid. In the summers, he'd sleep outside more than in his house. He's hunted rabbits and killed rattlesnakes. He's run over every mile of the backroads, day and night. He's fallen a couple of times, even landed on a lizard once that he thought was a snake. Scared the shit out of him." Another giggle. "But I guess it helps him to be out here. He says when he gets home, he goes right to sleep. That could mean only a couple hours of sleep, but it's all he needs. We're both grateful for that. He's had it tough since he's been home, but he's getting better."

"You don't think the lightning will bother him? Some vets I know can't be around fireworks, loud crowds or any kind of sudden noise."

"Maybe. He's run during other storms. I'm hoping he'll be okay in this one." She stared at the black space where her brother jogged. "But we can't bother him. We have to leave him alone."

"Shouldn't we give him a ride? He's got to be soaked."

"No, he can't know I brought you here. Don't say anything to George, okay? He'll have my head if he learns I let you in on his secret."

"If you say so . . . no problem."

"Please, keep it between us."

"Why all the secrecy? Why didn't George tell me? Or you?"

"George doesn't want anybody to know, except his kids and me. He's a private man, I told you that. As far as he's concerned, it's nobody's business what he does to take care of himself. I didn't tell you when I heard your story for the same reason, respect for George's sense of privacy. I told you now because I thought you should know, so that you won't think there was still something to clear up, especially with Mat coming home." She hiccuped and covered her mouth. "And maybe the wine got to me."

"Thanks, I guess. And that's who I saw that night I was out here?"

"Had to be, unless you believe in ghosts."

"Okay. Now I know the story behind the legend of the ghost of Running Elk."

"People were seeing Running Elk long before George started his nighttime runs. That's one mystery still unsolved."

"Not my kind of mystery. I'll leave that one to Sonny Baca."

"Who?"

"Rudy Anaya's detective. He was always chasing spirits and *brujas*, legends, myths. Good stories. You must've read at least one of his mystery books."

"Oh, right. I'd forgotten." Her eyes looked heavy.

"I better get you home. It's late and wet. Don't want to get stuck in the mud."

"Good idea."

"We gonna run into George?"

"No. He circles back around, in the other direction. He might see our lights, but that won't mean anything to him. He'll keep running until he gets back to his house. He's on one track out here. Total focus."

"All right. Let's go."

The rain eased up, and I fishtailed the pickup in the mud only a couple of times. Essie fell asleep to the rhythm of raindrops dancing on the truck's rusted metal. By the time I parked at her house, the storm was over, the stars had returned and one less ghost haunted me.

Nineteen

The next morning, before Essie or Felisa woke up, I was groggy as hell, but I couldn't stay in bed. I used my phone to send a long email to Corrine that included questions I wanted her to research. I pored over my notebook and wrote more notes to myself. When my stomach growled, I made a pot of oatmeal, and Essie joined me for a quick breakfast.

"My head hurts," she complained. "Never could drink wine. But I sure do like it."

"I'm that way about whiskey, bourbon. Gives me a rash on my chest, then the nastiest hangovers."

"And yet, we don't learn, do we?"

"What fun is that?"

She finished off her cereal. "I shouldn't've let you see George last night. I promised I wouldn't tell anyone. I regret it. He trusted me, and that's hard for him to do. If he finds out . . ."

"I'll never say a word. That's *my* promise."

"And I shouldn't've put you in that position. I'm sorry."

Before I could do much to ease her conscience, she left for several appointments that she'd delayed because of Mat's disappearance. I walked in circles around the house until Alicia showed up to watch over her sleeping grandmother.

My destination was the police building. I'd given up on Delgado the day before. I hated the idea, but I had to make another run at him. I couldn't let go of the gut feeling that he still had one or two pieces of information to reveal.

Delgado was a key to understanding the mystery of Matías Montoya, a mystery that went beyond the basic puzzle of a chronic runaway teenager. The writer slash con man had hidden facts and details about Mat from Chief López and me. He'd overreacted when he discovered that Mat's backpack was missing, as though the pack had been loaded with money or illegal drugs. He'd tried to scam the trusting people of Melton and, except for his botched hanging, he'd done nothing to indicate he had a guilty conscience about any of his actions. I doubted that he'd told me all that he knew about Mat, and I didn't have much confidence that what he'd told me was completely true.

My plan didn't make it past the first step.

"He posted bail," Chief López told me when I said I needed to talk with Delgado one more time. "Left last night, late."

"He had bail money?"

"Tanney bailed him out."

"Who the hell is Tanney?"

"Wermer Wilson Tanney. AKA Werm. You know that guy, don't you?"

"I've met him. One of the more colorful folk of Melton. What's his link to Delgado?"

"Can't say. All I know is that Werm called last night and asked about getting Delgado released if he brought in the bail money. It was only a thousand bucks. Easy enough for Werm. I had no reason to say no, so about nine o'clock Delgado and Werm walked out of here."

"Know where they were going?"

"Didn't ask, not my business once the bail was paid. But they only had a couple of choices. Delgado's trailer, which must be an even bigger mess since he hasn't been there for days. Or Werm's place. The Castle."

"Castle?"

"It's an old mansion built out of gray granite and prairie deadwood. Lots of dark wood inside. One corner is a tower that used to have a bell. Guess that's why it's called the Castle. Sits on a hill that overlooks the town. It's been the Castle since Werm's great-grandparents built it. It's starting to fall apart, but when Werm needs a place to sleep, that's where he goes. Home, sweet big old drafty home."

"I'll be damned. Turns out the two oddest ducks in Melton are friends."

López shook his head. "I wouldn't call them friends. When they left, they barely said two words to each other. I got the definite impression that Werm was doing something he didn't want to do. Or at least it wasn't his idea. Neither one looked happy."

"Then why did he do it?"

"Again, none of my business, and I didn't ask."

"Respect for privacy? I hear that's a big deal around here."

"That's right. This ain't the city, where everybody's business is on the street. There are a lot of reasons people choose to live out here. Keeping shit to yourself is right up there, along with fresh air. And no traffic or homeless camps."

I almost said *and no life*.

"So I've heard." And yet, the small-town contradiction couldn't be avoided. A healthy respect for privacy existed right along the undeniable fact that secrets didn't remain secret for long. *Must be part of the culture*, I thought.

I spent a few more minutes with the chief. I told him about the things bothering me, and he was polite as he listened. He didn't react, other than to remind me that Mat's family was expecting him any day. I left him in his hot, dreary office and drove through hot dreary Melton to Wes Delgado's trailer.

The bent door was halfway open. Mud and puddles of rain covered the trailer's floor. Small animals scurried away when I pushed the door completely open. They might have been mice. The place looked like a tornado had torn through it. One thing was clear. Wes Delgado was not at home.

I called Essie and asked her for directions to the Castle.

≫ ≫ ≫

The road to the Castle was made from crushed white rock. A thin plume of dust followed me as I drove up the hill to the house, which sat on the edge of a rise that offered an unobstructed view of the town and the surrounding empty landscape.

The summer heat had cranked up again. My truck labored up the hill and I worried that I'd pushed the pickup with the trip to Pueblo and my late night, rain-drenched drive to snoop on George. I didn't like the idea of walking back to Melton in the heat. I checked my phone's battery, just in case the truck gave out. Fifty percent. It would have to do.

Except for the hardened mud on my tires, there weren't any signs that a storm had passed through the previous night. The terrain looked dry, worn-out. Just like the town of Melton proper.

I tried to connect the dots between Delgado and Werm, but nothing stood out. With a bit of luck, I hoped to find the two men, and a few answers, in the Castle.

It didn't look promising as I parked in front of the massive ranch-style house. No other cars were in sight, and the place looked empty and pathetic. A round turret, made from black and brown boulders, poked up from one of the building's corners.

I eased out of my pickup and slowly made my way along the brick walkway, then up the sandstone steps to the wooden deck of the porch. The porch stretched across the entire front of the house. Except for a pair of overturned lawn chairs, the porch was empty.

The screen door was wedged open as though it had been stuck in place for a dozen years. Behind the screen door was a heavy gray slab, the actual door. I tried the doorknob, a miniature gargoyle made of brass, and the slab swung open.

I expected Delgado or Werm to jump out, waving a shotgun, and I entered the house with my eyes trying to take in everything at once, my legs ready to dodge whatever Delgado or Werm threw at me.

I slipped into the house and smelled dust, musty air and sour milk. The house was dark and cool.

The front part of the house contained a long dark dinner table with matching chairs. Gray sheets covered other pieces of furniture, and an old-fashioned portrait of a man with a handlebar mustache hung crookedly on one wall. I walked into the kitchen and righted an overturned milk carton. I smelled something else, smoky and metallic, that reminded me of the gunshots during the Pueblo raid.

I stopped walking and listened. I heard a moan coming from the hallway at the other end of the kitchen. I waited for a minute. The moaning continued. I moved as slowly as possible until I stuck my head through the kitchen archway and into the hallway.

Werm lay curled in a ball at the foot of the stairs that climbed to the tower. He looked unconscious, but the moaning came from him. Blood leaked from under his blood-soaked shirt and congealed in a pool at the stairs.

"Delgado!" I hollered up the stairs. "Come out. It's over!"

I didn't expect an answer, but I thought it was worth a shot. I tried to stop the blood oozing out of Werm's side by applying pressure with my left hand. With my right hand, I called López.

Twenty

López's Jeep slammed to a dusty stop twenty minutes later. Before the cloud of gravel and white dust settled, he ran into the house and made sure Werm was still alive. He told me he'd called the doctor and the Eads hospital, and that Freddy, the town bartender and volunteer deputy, should show up any minute to help me. He used first aid supplies he'd brought to help with the blood. Then he said he had to go.

"Delgado can't be too far away," he explained. "The shooting must've happened just before you arrived. Hell, Delgado might've seen you coming, and that's why he ran off. I've got to go after him."

"I didn't see anybody or any car on my way up here."

"The road continues on to the other side of the hill. Ends up in Kansas. It's the only way he could've gone if you didn't see him. I'll catch him, but I have to leave now."

His car raced over the top of the hill in another burst of gravel and white dust.

When Freddy arrived with Doctor Cleary, I released my hand from Werm's bloody side. I felt as though I'd been kneeling over the wounded man for weeks, sloshing in blood, listening to Werm's moans grow weaker with each labored breath.

"This man has lost a lot of blood," Cleary said.

That was obvious, but I guess he had to say something.

"Good thing you found him when you did." He whispered the words as though he didn't want me to hear them. "He could've bled out and died, and no one would've known for weeks. Nobody ever comes up here. If he lives, it's because of you."

He never looked at me while he spoke. He didn't acknowledge me in any meaningful way. I realized that the doctor and I had a bad habit of meeting over the prone bodies of unconscious, injured men.

"Just doing my job," I said. "You remember, I'm looking for Mat." I doubted he wanted to be reminded of our earlier conversation at his house, but I couldn't resist.

"That's why you came up here? Mat Montoya? I don't understand."

"That's okay, doc. Don't worry about it. You got your hands full."

I found a bathroom and washed my hands and arms and threw water in my face with the hope that it would wipe out the image of Werm's bloody body curled on the floor. I loosened my tight legs and cramped knees by walking through the house, but nothing grabbed my attention, nothing stayed with me. It was an old, forsaken house without memories, without any human presence.

A fine layer of white dust covered the floor and walls. The white dust seemed to be everywhere, like an extra coat of paint, hiding marks and scars from the history of the house. The Castle depressed me, so I waited on the porch in case Freddy or the doctor needed something.

In only a few days, Delgado had gone from suspected con man to attempted suicide to attempted murderer. I assumed that now he was being chased across the plains by every cop in eastern Colorado. It'd been a bad week for Wes Delgado, and an even worse one for Wermer Wilson Tanney.

Within five minutes of their arrival, Freddy and the doctor decided they needed to rush Werm to the hospital.

"We can't wait for the ambulance," Freddy said. "Doc says there's too much blood loss. Help me get him in my car."

Freddy and the doctor drove off with the unconscious man stretched on the back seat of Freddy's car. Freddy's final words to me were, "I hope he doesn't die in my car." The doctor didn't say anything. I walked through the house again, and this time the smell

of blood hit me. I made my way around the bloody floor and
climbed the stairs to the tower.

The oval room had a bed, dresser and a chair. Shirts and pants
hung on a clothes rack. A mirror took up space on one wall, and a
ceramic sink protruded from the opposite corner. A series of small
windows ringed the room, offering a view of the town and a hundred surrounding miles of the flat Colorado landscape and the
not-so-distant Kansas border. Except for faint traces of the white
dust, the room was in better shape than the rest of the house. The
only object that looked out-of-place was an overflowing ashtray.

Next to the mirror, a half-dozen framed photographs clung to
the wall. They were old photographs that I assumed were pictures
of the Tanney family at Tanney get-togethers. Because it was different, one black-and-white held my attention. It was a five-by-eight
group photo of two dozen men and women dressed in suits and
shiny dresses. A few raised glasses of what I assumed was cham-
pagne, others held noisemakers and wore paper hats. A sign on the
wall behind the group proclaimed HAPPY NEW YEAR! I didn't
see any indication of which year was being celebrated. I scanned
the people in the picture—all white, projecting wealth and influ-
ence, giddy with material success—until I recognized the face of
Annie Cleary, the doctor's wife. She was several years younger, but
I was sure it was her. A man to her left, dressed in a tuxedo and
bowtie, had his arm over her shoulder. It was Robert Cleary, the
doctor, also much younger. The pair smiled at the camera. To the
woman's right, Werm looked uneasy, unsmiling. He was staring at
the doctor, not the camera, but it was him.

Three old friends, celebrating at the club, I thought. *Nothing
unusual about that.*

Twenty-one

Essie, George, Felisa and Alicia waited for me at Essie's house. No surprise. They already knew about the shooting at the Castle.

"Is it true?" George said when I walked through the front door. "Delgado killed Werm? Why? What's happening?"

"Werm's not dead," I answered. "At least he wasn't when Freddy and Cleary took him to Eads. Not unless you've heard something new."

They shook their heads.

I told the assembled Montoya family everything I knew about the day's events, beginning with my wasted trip to the jail and ending with Freddy's cynical hope that Delgado wouldn't die in his car. Felisa made the sign of the cross when she heard Freddy's words.

My story resulted in many more questions from them, and I answered all that I could. The most difficult was trying to explain why I'd driven to Werm's house in the first place, although Essie commented that it was lucky for Werm that I had.

"I think Delgado knows more about Mat's disappearance than he's let on," I said. "He's lied several times about Mat and his relationship to him. We still don't know the reason he tried to kill himself, although I tend to agree with Chief López that Delgado was finished, tapped out. I wanted to pin him down, just in case." I ended abruptly. I couldn't say what I should've said.

"In case of what?" George asked. His eyes were closed as he asked the question. He sensed my doubts about Mat coming home.

"Gus is just trying to tie up all the loose ends, George," Essie said.

"Is that right, Gus?" George asked, his eyes still shut.

"Yes, that's right. Loose ends and, uh . . . and I wanted to be ready if there are any glitches or delays with Mat coming home.

Mat could easily change his mind and we'll be back where we started. I wanted to be ready to go look for him, know where to
continue with my search. I think Delgado can be a lead for that."

Essie nodded. George opened his eyes and let out his breath.
My answer made sense to them, and even to me.

"Thanks for not giving up, Gus," George said. "When Mat's
home, I promise that we'll treat you and a guest to one of Freddy's
burger deluxe specials at the Sand Creek Saloon. The best Melton
has to offer. I promise."

They all laughed, Felisa the loudest. George grinned and put
on a good front, but he soon excused himself. He said he was tired
and had to finish up a few small jobs in his shop. He took Alicia
with him, and five minutes later only Essie and I remained in the
living room.

"You don't think Mat's coming home, do you?" Essie asked.

"I'm not quitting, if that's what you're thinking. But we should
be prepared for anything."

"But the text messages. We all saw those. If they weren't from
Mat, then who? And why?"

"I don't know, Essie, but I'm working on it. Corrine's helping,
up in Denver. Her activist work for the community . . . the groups
she belongs to, the meetings she attends . . . she has resources,
friends who can provide information. She moves in a world of
favors . . . favors she does for others, and favors owed to her. A few
more days, maybe I'll have something concrete, something I can
use, some answers."

She frowned. "If Mat didn't send the texts, then whoever did is
cruel, mean," she said. "Those messages are the only thing we've
had to pin our hopes on. If they're not real…" Her voice trailed off.

Her cell phone buzzed, and her body shuddered. She listened
for several seconds, then said, "Okay, Rob. Thanks for calling." She
listened again. "Yes, he's right here. I'll tell him." She ended the call.

"What's up? The Chief arrest Delgado?"

"Not exactly. Rob said he caught up to Delgado, but he wouldn't stop. Rob chased him for several miles on the highway. He called the State Patrol and had them set up a roadblock in front of the bridge across Mule Deer Creek, almost at the border. But Delgado never slowed down. Rob said it looked like he was going to crash through the roadblock, and the state cops were ready to stop him with bullets. At the last minute, Delgado swerved off the road, flew through the air and crashed into a pile of boulders in the dry creek bed."

"Jesus," I said.

"He's dead," Essie continued. "Rob said he thought Delgado did it on purpose. He finally succeeded in killing himself."

※ ※ ※

The death of Wes Delgado ended my investigation into the disappearance of Mat Montoya . . . or so I thought. I'd counted on Delgado knowing more than he'd revealed, and I'd concluded that those revelations—if I could wrench them from Delgado—would provide me with enough information to keep me in the search. But a dead Delgado meant a dead end for me.

Werm was an obvious source to check out, but he was in a drug-induced coma in the ICU at Parkview Medical Center in Pueblo, where a flight-for-life helicopter had taken him when the Eads hospital staff admitted they couldn't do anything more for the critically injured man. The bullet damaged his lungs, and he required a ventilator to keep breathing. No one could say how long he would be out, or whether he would survive. He was the only person who knew what had happened, why he'd bailed out Delgado and why Delgado shot him, but he sure wasn't talking now and there was no guarantee that he would talk when, and if, he regained consciousness. The people of Melton valued their privacy, as I'd been reminded more than once. That might include not explaining why you were shot by the man you bailed out of jail.

And there was Corrine. She might dig up something that would put me back on the case, but I didn't hear anything from her the night we learned of Delgado's death. The next day also passed without a word. The trail dried up, and I had no place to go except Denver. I said that to George and Essie, and they didn't try to talk me into staying longer. No one mentioned that Mat was supposed to be coming home. I think we'd all reached a dead end.

The night before my return trip to Denver, George asked me to take my pickup into his shop. He wanted to give it a once-over to satisfy himself that it would finish the journey. I stayed while he worked; oil change, lube, tire check, brake inspection, carburetor cleaning and so on. He replaced some parts, greased and oiled others, and told me to invest in a new set of tires when I returned to the city.

During the tune-up, I summed up what I knew about Mat, which he'd already heard, but he said it made him feel better to know the details of Mat's last visit to Pueblo and then the unusual meeting with Delgado, when the backpack was dropped off. He listened and occasionally nodded, all while working.

When he finished, he suggested we wash the truck, so I helped hose off the soap he used on the mud-caked tires.

"This mud's from out by the bluffs, ain't it?" he asked.

"Could be. There's mud all over around here. Mud or white dust."

"You must've picked it up the night you and Essie were out there. That was a downpour, for sure."

"You saw us?"

"Of course. You were parked about ten feet from me. Even in the dark, in a rainstorm, I can still see a pickup that's ten feet away."

"You didn't say anything."

"Nothing to say. I don't doubt that Essie had a good reason for taking you out there, letting you in on my little secret. It's okay, cuz. No harm, no problem."

"I'm sorry, George."

"Really, it's all right. I've decided I don't care who knows I run around the boonies at night. People around here do much weirder shit than that. You've seen some of it. All I'm doing is exercise, taking care of myself, trying to get to sleep. Keeping alive the legend of Running Elk, so to speak. It doesn't bother me who knows that. I'll have to talk with Essie . . . clear the air with her. She's probably carrying a ton of guilt about what she did. I'll let her off the hook."

He finished working on my pickup and told me he felt confident that my ride was in surprisingly good shape for the trip home.

"How much I owe you for the overhaul, the tune-up?" I asked. I pulled out my wallet.

"Put that away, cuz. It's on me, the least I can do."

"No way. You don't have to do that."

"If anything, I owe you money. What's the final bill for your services?"

"I'm not charging you, you're family. Besides, I didn't find Mat. No result, no charge."

He pulled out a folded check from his shirt pocket, unfolded it and tried to hand it to me. "You worked for me, I owe you," he said. "That's the way this works. I hope this covers it"

"I won't take it."

He glared at me, and for an instant I thought I would see the side of George that I'd heard about but never experienced.

"Tell you what," I said before the situation deteriorated any further. "Let's call it even. You put my truck in shape, made it safe to drive again. In Denver, we'd be talking big bucks for a mechanic's time. That's more than enough payment for the little I did. I think anyone would agree. We're square, George. Okay? Leave it at that."

He refolded the check, slipped it back into his shirt pocket and offered his hand to shake. I took it. He pulled me close and hugged me.

"Thank you, Gus. I mean it. Thank you."

On the way to Essie's house, the pickup sounded clean, reborn. I felt good driving it, and I promised myself that I would buy the tires George recommended, and that I'd finally paint the truck.

Off to the northeast, lightning flashed and thunder rolled. The storm appeared to be centered over the Dead Snake Bluffs, the same area that had been pummeled by rain, hail and wind for several afternoons and nights. The rain hit before I arrived at Essie's, and I had to run from the truck to her front door in solid water. I was dripping wet when I entered the house.

Essie stood in darkness in the middle of her front room. She held a phone to her ear with shaking hands. Tears welled up in her eyes. She nodded at me, then told the person she was talking to that she would call him back.

Lightning spotlighted the house, and thunder shook the windows.

She couldn't say the words.

"What's wrong?" I said.

The intermittent lightning bursts streaked her face with white flashes.

"That was Leroy. He's out on the bluffs, looking for calves spooked by the storm. Strays. He said the ground is soaked, and some of the bluffs have fallen apart. He said, he said . . ."

"What. Essie? What did he say?"

"He said he thinks he's found a body up there. Human remains, he called it. Uncovered by the storms. He wanted me to know." She dropped her phone and fell back on the couch.

Twenty-two

The temperature reached one hundred and one by the time Mat's funeral ended. Dressed in a suit and tie, I felt every degree. Hundreds of people crowded around the gravesite, where we sweated in the dizzying heat. An older man passed out, followed by a pregnant woman. Children languished in the shade of a lone tree. Babies whimpered, women fanned themselves, men wiped the backs of their necks with handkerchiefs. Several faces were tear stained. For days, the news stories focused on Mat's disappearance, his apparent murder and the "desperate chase and deadly crash," as the *Pueblo Chieftain* put it. Although the family asked for privacy, the headline voyeurs and morbidly curious showed up in droves.

At the head of the crowd, near the casket, Corrine and Max stood with me next to Essie and Felisa, while George and Alicia were directly in front of us. My sisters had come in one car from Denver. Corrine had no current boyfriend, and Sandra, Max's wife, was on the road with The Rakers, the band that Max managed. We suffered through the heat, except for Felisa, who watched passively with her ever-present shawl draped across her shoulders. Somewhere in the throng, Toni Marriot and Jeannie from Pueblo also mourned. Connor and members of Mat's high school class served as pallbearers. I assumed that most of Melton was in attendance, and I mentally checked names off my list of Melton people I personally knew: Chief López, the Cleary family, Leroy Bannon, Susan O'Brien, Connor, Freddy the bartender and part-time cop, the Montoyas. Only Werm and Delgado were missing.

It had been a nightmare week.

Mat's remains were identified through his DNA, but George demanded that he be allowed to look at his son. All of us told him not to do it, but there was no stopping George. Afterwards, he had to be escorted from the mortuary by Essie and Alicia. He wouldn't talk to any of us for more than a few minutes, and Essie feared he'd end up in a hospital.

Mat's official cause of death was listed as trauma from a blow to the head. That could've happened in a fall at the bluffs or from someone hitting Mat. It did look as though the body had been buried in the bluffs and that the grave had caved in with the rain. The County Medical Examiner called the death and surrounding circumstances "inconclusive." The unofficial cause of death, believed by Chief López and everyone else in Melton, was that Wes Delgado had killed Mat and shot Werm. What no one could agree about was why Delgado did it.

"They were into something shady," López said when I asked him about Delgado's motive. "I mean Werm and Delgado, not Mat."

We stood in the street and waited for George, Essie and Alicia to exit the mortuary.

"No honor among thieves. Maybe Werm tried to scam the scammer, maybe Delgado double-crossed Werm. It'll be something like that, but we have to wait for Werm to come around. He'll tell us what was going on with Delgado. He won't have a choice."

I wasn't as sure that Werm would say anything. His posting bail for the con man put Werm in the category of person of interest. That meant it was unlikely we'd get the full story from him. But maybe the fact that he'd almost been killed by Delgado would motivate him to explain what happened between the two.

I returned to Denver for a few days between the discovery and the services, but that didn't feel right. I drove Corrine crazy with my questions and doubts. When we finally had a full-blown no-holds-barred argument, I gassed up my truck and drove back to Melton to help in any way I could. It came down to me spending time with George. I listened as he bragged about his son and condemned himself for the mistakes he'd made as a father. I tried to tell him that he was a good father, but George wasn't ready to hear that.

Essie, with help from Alicia and Felisa, coordinated the arrangements for Mat's funeral, as well as a reception in the church basement. She'd feared that the expected crowd of strangers would ruin the reception, but Chief López and his two deputies waited at the back door to the church, which also served as the entryway to the basement hall. They turned away anyone who wasn't a relative, friend or from Melton, including a pair of reporters from Denver television stations.

I'd been to several funerals and receptions, starting when I was a kid, for my grandparents, and lasting through the unexpected deaths of my parents when I was fourteen and fifteen. These events usually followed a pattern, and Mat's services kept to the blueprint. The day began with a Mass at the small Catholic church, where Essie and Connor said a few words about Mat, then the mourners followed the hearse to the cemetery. More prayers at the graveside, and another drive back to the church for the reception. A priest opened the reception with a prayer, Essie expressed gratitude from the family for the people who gathered to remember and honor Mat, and everyone lined up for food served cafeteria style. Usually, about half-way through the meal, people were more relaxed, and typically the conversation turned to memories of happier days and even humorous stories about the deceased.

Some of that happened at Mat's reception, but most of the guests weren't going to relax, and there wouldn't be many funny stories about Mat. The violent death of one of Melton's children had rocked the town, and the shock hadn't worn off. The sadness from the cemetery stayed with the crowd through the afternoon.

George left the reception before it was finished. Essie told Alicia and Felisa to go with him, and Connor volunteered to help. Shortly after they left, the crowd thinned out and I ended up sitting at a table with Essie, Corrine, Max, Toni Marriot and Jeannie.

Near the door, the Clearys—the doctor, Annie *and* Yvonne—sat with the teacher, Susan O'Brien. In another corner, Rob López, Leroy Bannon and Freddy drank coffee. A few other tables were taken up by families of some of Mat's fellow students, including Joe and Clara Darby, Connor's parents.

Jeannie asked me about Mat's girlfriend. I pointed at the table where Yvonne sat with her parents. Jeannie stared at the girl.

"Are the Clearys friends of the teacher?" I asked Essie.

"They're family. She's their niece. Her father is Annie Cleary's brother."

"Small world."

"I told you that, didn't I? That day we talked to her?"

"You probably did. I forget stuff."

She shook her head. "You're a lot better than when you first got here. Don't you think so?" She looked at Corrine and Max.

"I was going to say the same thing," Max said. "You're in better shape than the last time I saw you. Right, Corrine?"

My older sister raised the cup of lemonade she'd been drinking. "Here's to Gus. I'm happy to see more of the brother I remember. I only wish it was under more positive circumstances."

The rest of us raised our glasses of lemonade or coffee.

"For Mat," I said. "From what I've learned about him, he was quite a guy. I'm proud to be related."

I chugged the tasteless lemonade and waited for someone else to make a toast. Life had become scripted and predictable. We went through the motions, did what we needed to do, but I remember hearing, more than once, "It doesn't feel real," and no one disagreed.

"And with that, we have to go," Toni said. "Long ride back to Pueblo."

I walked them to Toni's car. It hadn't been the reunion we wanted, but I was glad she had made the trip, and I told her so. She gave me a hug and reminded me to look her up when I returned to Pueblo. She climbed in her car and waited for Jeannie.

That's when Mat's fellow runaway fell apart. The tears came fast and full, and for several minutes Toni and I let her expel the demon of grief she carried for Mat. Between tears and hiccups, she talked about Mat and their time together. Her disjointed memories were about insignificant things that were important only to her, but the girl's pain hit me full on. I staggered under the weight of the grief created by Mat's death.

For a second, I couldn't breathe. I grabbed Jeannie's hand and squeezed it. The girl held on, and together we shared a moment of peace. She stepped back and took a deep breath. I did the same.

The Clearys and the teacher walked by as Jeannie pulled herself together. The doctor nodded at me, and I nodded back.

"That girl, Yvonne? Not what I expected," she said, with only a hint of jealousy.

She went on for another minute or two about Mat and his broken heart and the girl from his hometown. I listened closely, unaware of the irony in my gratitude for memories of a boy I never knew. Finally, Jeannie climbed into Toni's car, and they drove off for Pueblo.

Back in the hall, I suggested and then everyone joined in about doing something special to honor Mat. Essie was excited about that idea and wanted to talk with me about such a project, "sometime real soon." More goodbyes were said twenty minutes later. Corrine, Max and I helped collect the trash and sweep the basement hall, then we hugged Essie and left our cousin with promises that we would keep in touch

Corrine and Max wanted me to follow them on the trip to Denver, so we agreed that they would wait for me at the gas station after I checked on George one more time.

"We'll be waiting," Corrine yelled at me from her car. "We need to be on the road before it gets dark."

I was almost at George's house, when my phone buzzed. The ID said it was George Montoya.

"Hey, George. What's up?" I thought he might be calling to cancel my visit.

"Can you drop by? I want to talk with you about something. It's important."

"Uh, yeah, sure. I'm on my way. You okay?"

His call was unnecessary. We'd agreed at the reception that I would come by his house before I hit the road.

"I'm good. I'm good. Never better. You'll be here soon, then?"

Strange answer. Even George knew he was not good. He'd said as much at the reception. And never better? On the day he buried his son?

"Five minutes. Anything in particular?"

"Running Elk called. He wants an answer. He's kind of impatient."

"Tell the old Indian to hold his horses." I hoped I sounded like I knew what he was talking about. "I'll take care of him, he knows that."

George hung up. I drove for a few minutes more. When George's house came into view, I pulled to the side of the road, parked the truck and called Rob López.

"Chief," I said to his voicemail, "George is in trouble, at his house. Not sure what's going on. I'm there now. Get up here as fast as you can."

I was about a hundred yards from the house. There were at least four people with George: Alicia, Felisa, Connor, and number four was whoever had caused George to talk gibberish about Running Elk. The afternoon sun was still high and bright, so there was no way for me to sneak up to the house without being seen. I'd be exposed, a target. Number four wanted me at George's; there was no other reason for George to call. *Did number four want to talk, or would he shoot me as soon as I stood in the road?*

Paranoia slipped over the edge of my awareness. *What if the person in the house was Mat's killer, and the Montoya family, including me, was next on the list of victims? What if George had lost it complete-*

*ly and was planning on ending the life of the investigator who'd failed
to save Mat? What if . . .*

I forced myself to quit thinking that way and decided I didn't
have a choice. I couldn't wait for López. George and the others
were at risk and more likely to be hurt the longer I stayed outside
the house. I didn't know what the odds were, or whether I'd get
further than the front of my truck before a bullet stopped me per-
manently. Hell, I didn't know what I would do if I made it into the
house. I took off my suit coat, removed the tie from around my
neck and wiped my sweating face one more time.

I opened the driver's side door, climbed out and walked in the
middle of the road. I tried to be casual and to walk without betray-
ing my anxiety. My perspiration-stained white shirt gleamed in the
sunlight and contrasted sharply with my skin. I was a brilliant,
obvious, slow-moving target.

A pair of gray and green lizards skittered at the edge of the
road. A pale daytime moon quivered in the hazy summer sky. The
rocks and cactus in George's front yard looked artificial, like low-
budget movie props. Nothing seemed real except the nervous lump
in my gut. I licked my lips and tasted salt. I wiped my forehead and
ran my sweaty fingers through my sweaty hair. I concentrated on
the door and window and watched for any movement.

I couldn't shake the feeling of *déjà vu*. In Pueblo, I'd walked
into a similar scene: Scuggins threatened innocents, and I was
forced to act without a clear idea of what I should do. Toni had
saved the day in Pueblo. Unfortunately, she wasn't waiting in
George's house.

I stepped up onto the porch and knocked on the door. George
answered. His face was bruised and cut. Dried blood marked
swollen lips.

"Come in, Gus."

I didn't see anyone else in the room behind him. George
stepped back from the door. His eyes drifted in tandem to his right.
Then his entire body moved.

"Chuy! Coco!" he shouted as he threw himself on the floor.

Without thinking through what I was doing, I jumped across the threshold past George, turned as sharp as I could and ducked. The dogs rushed in behind me, tumbled across George, then yipped and barked, snapping their jaws. From the edge of the room, Randolph Scuggins, distracted by the dogs for an instant, shot at me as I dived behind the couch. The bullet lodged in the wall above my head, spraying plaster. A second shot immediately followed, then the crash of a lamp and finally a loud thud.

"You okay, Gus?" George hollered.

I looked over the edge of the back of the couch. George was on all fours. The dogs had retreated behind George, where they snarled at Scuggins. He was squirming and moaning on the floor, surrounded by shards of a broken lamp and the gun he'd dropped. Blood oozed from a shattered shoulder. Off to the left, Felisa Montoya sat in her wheelchair and aimed George's hunting rifle at the wounded Scuggins.

"Never better," I hollered back.

Twenty-three

Randolph Scuggins never had a chance. He had a plan to retaliate for my role in his arrest, but it was doomed from the instant it hatched in his tormented imagination. He had followed George and his passengers from the reception, stormed into the house with pistol held high and demanded that George talk me into driving to the house. He bragged to George that he was going to hurt me, bad, and then finish me off, "as slow as possible." George said Scuggins laughed about the various kinds of pain and damage he intended to inflict on me.

He herded Felisa, Alicia and Connor into a corner and focused on George. After all, what could an old crippled woman and two frightened teenagers do?

He didn't know that Felisa had handled guns her entire life, including when she was the girlfriend and unofficial deputy of the sheriff of Lincoln County, New Mexico, and that Alicia and Connor were members of the Melton High School Rifle Club.

When George wouldn't make the phone call, Scuggins resorted to the only persuasive tactic he knew, assaulting the victim. He punched George several times, and when George still refused, Scuggins used the butt of his pistol. Blood streamed from George's forehead, but there was nothing Scuggins could do that would've made George lead me into a trap.

Felisa, Alicia and Connor demanded, then begged Scuggins to stop beating George. In desperation, Alicia screamed, "Leave my father alone! I'll make the call. Quit hurting him!" That's all Scuggins needed.

"Make the call or I start in on your daughter," Scuggins said to George.

At that point, George had no choice and he called me.

Scuggins watched George like a rattler watches a diving red-tailed hawk. He wasn't worried about the others and glanced at them only briefly, without really seeing them. When George connected with me, Scuggins had eyes and ears only for George's side of the phone call. Felisa slipped the rifle from its rack and covered it with her shawl. While Scuggins tried to understand what George said about a running elk, Alicia plucked a bullet from the box George kept behind the rack and slipped it to her grandmother. Felisa took care of the rest.

Scuggins lived, but his shooting meant that I had to stay in Melton for a few more days, and that Corrine and Max drove to Denver a day later than planned without me as an escort.

I'd been warned about Scuggins. Two days after Mat's body was identified, Detective Grossman from Pueblo had called me.

"I thought you'd want to know," he said. "Randolph Scuggins worked out a deal with the feds, and we had to go along with it."

"He's gonna testify, so they put him in witness protection?"

"Something like that, but not quite. The feds want his boss, of course, or bosses maybe. They planned to use Scuggins to set up a meeting where the boss, *el jefe*, would incriminate himself and his organization."

"Sounds like someone's been watching too many Netflix movies."

"Tell me about it. But that's not the worst."

"Do I really want to know?"

"Yeah, you need to be aware. The feds turned him loose in Chicago, where the meeting was supposed to take place."

"Let me guess. They lost him."

"Of course."

"He's on the run?"

"Yeah. We figure he's headed for Texas, but he hasn't been seen since he gave the FBI the slip. But right around the time that he disappeared, the story broke about your nephew's body being found. That was the biggest story in Pueblo. The only story."

Mat wasn't my nephew, but I didn't correct Grossman. "You think Scuggins saw the story, too?"

"I'd bet on it. It made the national news. Whether he did or not, he's not the type of guy who'd forget about your role in his arrest. I'd be calling to warn you even if the kid hadn't been found. But with all the press about the body and the chase and the wreck in the desert, he's got to figure that he can find you in Melton. He knows you're part of the family."

"Yeah, I told him that myself. And I'm likely to be at the funeral."

"Right."

"So, I should watch my back."

"That'd be my advice."

"Thanks, detective. I'll keep that in mind."

After the wounded Scuggins was arrested by Grossman and hauled back to Pueblo, a pair of FBI agents interviewed me, but they looked and sounded bored. They decided to cut their losses and gave up trying to use Scuggins. The feds officially dropped behind the state of Colorado in their interest in Scuggins, which meant that upfront he faced an abundance of state charges and, ultimately, he'd be prosecuted for the federal crimes he'd committed.

Detective Grossman wasn't surprised that Scuggins had "screwed the pooch," as he put it. "Some guys learn from their fuck-ups," Grossman said. "Scuggins seems to just get dumber. He's gonna do a lot of hard time in Colorado." Scuggins was taken to the same Pueblo hospital where Werm remained in a coma. Grossman assured me that the Texan wasn't going anywhere except a Pueblo jail cell, and then to one of the state prisons.

Rob López took his turn asking me questions, and he also enjoyed a good laugh at Scuggins' expense. "Lucky for you the Montoyas are gun freaks, right?"

"And that they didn't lose it when Scuggins pulled his bullshit," I added. "They're strong people."

"Too bad about Mat," López said, suddenly serious. "He was just as strong. Smart. I thought, all in all, that he was a good kid, working out some issues, yeah, but that boy had quite a future waiting for him. What a waste."

That's when I ran my idea by the chief.

"You think people would be interested in doing something for Mat, something to keep his memory alive around here? Something that the family can help with, maybe the school, even your cop friends in Pueblo? Mat impressed a lot of folks. He was always helping someone. He took a risk by helping those people in Pueblo. And he didn't get anything out of it."

"What do you mean? What can be done?"

"I'm not totally sure. My sisters came up with the general idea, then they gave me a few suggestions. A scholarship fund in his name would be nice. I like that concept. Or maybe something for the kids at The Rising Sun in Pueblo. He was one of those kids. They remember him. I don't know what would have to be done, but maybe the people from Melton can get together and come up with something."

"George okay with this? You have to respect his—"

"Privacy. Yeah, I know. I've talked with him, he's all for it. So are Essie and the rest of the family. In fact, Essie suggested that the town council meet to discuss the idea."

"That would be the way to go," López said. "George is on the council, as well as Doctor Cleary, Leroy Bannon, me . . . a few others. If Essie likes the idea, then I'm okay with it, and the rest of the Council will be, too. If you want to make a presentation, we can have a meeting anytime."

"That quick? Don't people need notice?"

"You really aren't from around here, are you?"

"You've said that before."

"I can call everyone on the council, have a meeting in a day or two. It's no big deal. This isn't downtown Denver. For some of the members, the only issue will be how much it'll cost them. Mat might've been a special kid, but that doesn't mean everyone on the council is ready to open their wallets for him. Hate to be blunt, but that's the way it is."

"We can work on that. The first meeting is for brainstorming. Invite the town, anyone who is interested. We'll talk through ideas, see which one makes the most sense for Melton and the Montoya family."

"Yeah, we can do that." He paused, smiled. "Tell you the truth, I'm surprised you want to do something. I thought you were the hard detective from Denver. Didn't think you'd have a soft spot for a boy you never met."

I shrugged. "Family. That's all I can say. And so far, it's just an idea. We'll see what comes of it, if anything."

Twenty-four

I spent another night and then the next day at Essie's house. By late afternoon, I sat in the backyard, where the heat and light transported me into a vague state of inertia. I was surrounded by details and minutiae left over from my investigation into the disappearance of Matías Montoya. Corrine sent me the research she'd gathered from friends and people who owed her. I had my own notes and questions . . . questions that remained unanswered, no matter how many times I asked them. A small pile of photos of Mat and George reminded me that I had to return them to George.

The Melton High School yearbook lay open to two colorful pages of photographs of Mat's classmates. The theme for the pages was *A Day in the Life*. According to the yearbook text, only a dozen students made up the class that included Mat, Connor and Yvonne. The camera had captured Mat standing by a blackboard. A backpack rested on a chair next to the blackboard. Another photo showed the girls' volleyball team in a match against a team from Springfield. The last picture framed Connor and Yvonne holding hands as they walked down the main hall of the school. I looked hard at those photos. I hoped that if I saw Mat as his friends saw him, I could fight off the ugly images that kept coming at me. It was a useless hope.

I was interrupted by a call from Chief López. He confirmed that the town council meeting was scheduled for seven p.m. in the same church basement where we'd remembered Mat after his funeral. López said he expected George, Doctor Cleary, Leroy Bannon, Joe Darby and Susan O'Brien. "She's substituting for Gloria Ahern, the high school principal. Gloria's on vacation, Hawaii. Must be nice."

"Essie will be there, too," I said. "Anyone else?"

"It's a public meeting, so anyone can attend. But it'll be your show. You ready?"

"Guess I have to be."

≫ ≫ ≫

By the time Essie and I arrived, a crowd of two dozen people had gathered for the meeting. The church basement held the day's heat, so we propped open the door in case a breeze drifted by. That was another useless hope.

The council sat at a large conference table at one end of the hall. I didn't see Susan O'Brien. The audience squirmed on folding chairs lined up in rows facing the table. Alicia and Connor sat in the last row. Essie and I were told by the chief that he would call the meeting to order, then turn it over to us to explain what we wanted to do. He'd saved two chairs in the front row for us.

The meeting started a few minutes late. Chief López quickly turned to Essie and asked her to provide more details.

She thanked everyone for coming to the meeting and, on behalf of the family, she expressed gratitude for the support shown by the residents of Melton. At that point, George interrupted to add his thanks and appreciation. He spoke for only a couple of minutes. When he leaned back in his chair, Essie picked up where she'd left off.

She talked about Mat as only a loving aunt can talk about a favorite nephew. She summarized his short life and his accomplishments, including the various awards he'd won in school and his attempt to help victims of trafficking, but she was most animated when she described his sense of humor, his hunger for news about the world and his drive to learn new things, explore new ideas. She brought Mat back to life with her words of praise and love.

While she talked, a few more people entered the hall, including Susan O'Brien. López waved at her to take a seat at the table. She shook her head and leaned against the back wall.

Essie finished with her announcement that the family would establish a scholarship fund in Mat's name for a Melton student who planned to attend college.

"George and I have agreed to donate ten thousand dollars to get the fund started," she said. "If we can help another student achieve . . . uh . . . achieve that . . ."

She stopped. She tried to catch her breath, but the words wouldn't come. The full impact of what she said overwhelmed her. She started to cry. George walked to her side, hugged her and helped her back to her chair.

"Gus?" George said. "Maybe you can finish for Essie?"

I stood up, centered myself in front of the crowd. "If the town council will formally approve it, that will help considerably with the fundraising. It will go a long way to convincing other towns and school districts to participate."

I answered a few questions from the audience and the council. Finally, Leroy Bannon made a motion and the council voted to formally approve town sponsorship of the Mat Montoya Scholarship Fund. George abstained from voting, and Susan O'Brien used Gloria Ahern's proxy to vote for the fund.

The meeting ended shortly after the vote, and the crowd slowly thinned out. That's when I asked the council members to stay for a few minutes more.

"I have some questions and details I want to clear up before I go back to Denver," I said to López when he asked why I wanted the council to stay.

"You should've done that in the meeting," he said.

"Just a few minutes. Won't take long."

He shook his head and mumbled something about a pain in the ass. Then he had the council and Essie sit down again at the table.

I stood before an important group of people, the people who were responsible for maintaining the town of Melton, Colorado. A small town, to be sure, but someone had to deal with water and electricity, sewer pipes, police protection, street signs, school build-ings. Someone had to make decisions, give orders and keep the wheels turning.

When this group of important people looked at me, what did they see? Unimportant Gus Corral from Denver. A short Mexican with buzzed hair, faded jeans and a wrinkled shirt. They saw a guy with a bruised and dented forehead and a scarred collection of remnants of a violent past. When they listened to me, they heard insecurity and hesitation. Hell, I heard those things in my words as I said them. They hoped I wasn't a gang member, but they didn't know for sure. Doubt about whether I was a professional investi-gator—a professional anything—had to gnaw at the patience they showed me out of respect for George and Essie.

I stood in front of them with waning confidence, and I worried that my scrambled head would let me down and I would sink into a pathetic puddle of incoherence. A baseball bat to the head can have that effect.

But I moved ahead with my plan, such as it was. At that moment, in the hot and stuffy church basement, with a group of people who had no reason to trust me, I had no choice but to shake up the small world of Melton, Colorado.

Twenty-five

"Thanks for staying," I said. "This won't take long. I want to wrap up a few things about Mat. Things that I didn't want to talk about in the meeting. These may seem obvious to some of you. I'm good at stating the obvious. Just let me get through this, so I can tell George that I've finally finished my work for him."

"Get on with it, Gus," López said. "Some of us have things to do."

Bannon and Darby grunted agreement with the chief.

"All right, all right." I nodded at George.

He returned the nod, leaned back in his chair and kept his eyes on his fellow council members.

"I'll start by saying that I don't think Mat died from an accident. The medical examiner didn't rule that out, but I have, and so have most of you."

No one disagreed.

"George hired me to find Mat. Unfortunately, that never happened. But I did find out a lot *about* Mat. Some of what I learned, you heard tonight. Smart. Ambitious. Mature. Great kid. So great that it was difficult to put together a valid reason why someone would harm him. The Pueblo traffickers, maybe. But the Pueblo police don't think that. On the other hand, no one from Melton had an apparent reason to hurt Mat."

"That's right," Leroy Bannon said. "Mat didn't make enemies, only friends."

"Yet, from the beginning of my time here in Melton, I assumed the worst."

López shook his head. He'd consistently told me that Mat was okay. Did he think I was digging at him?

"I had to," I continued. "Sorry, George and Essie. I thought the unthinkable, hoped for the best, but no one had a motive to hurt Mat, not even Wes Delgado, the man blamed for killing Mat, and the man who can't defend himself."

"Come on, Gus," López said. "You're actually doing this?" He stood up and paced behind the Council. "You gonna make a big reveal about the killer? Is that what this is? You think somebody in this room killed Mat? You playing Sherlock Holmes? I really don't have time for this. Delgado killed Mat, and Wermer Tanney will confirm that. You can't be serious about somebody else being responsible."

Essie looked worried, as though I'd gone too far again. The people at the table glanced at each other, uncertainty on their faces. For a second, I thought the meeting was over.

"Please hear him out," Essie said. "It's the least we can do for Mat."

"Essie's right, chief," Bannon said. It was predictable that he'd side with Essie. "Let him talk. He's got my attention. Let's hear where he's going with this."

Darby and George nodded in agreement. López returned to his chair at the table.

"Do it," López said. "But quickly."

I cleared my throat. "First, the puzzle of Wes Delgado. Con man? No doubt. Killer? I don't think so. But he wasn't above doing some very shady things. For Delgado, money was the end-all-be-all. He needed it, he didn't have much and he would do just about anything to get it. What really caught my attention was his reaction to losing Mat's backpack. He absolutely crumbled when he learned that the pack had been stolen. He tried to kill himself. But he wasn't upset because he'd failed to protect the pack that had been left in his care by Mat. He didn't have that sense of responsibility. He didn't tell Chief López about the pack, and he told me only when he realized that his blackmail scheme was in jeopardy. He saw me as an alternative, a link to Mat's family and another potential source of money."

"Blackmail?" López shouted. "What in the hell are you talking about?"

"I'm getting there. Believe it or not, I think Delgado had a touch of conscience, a twinge of guilt. He wanted to give me the backpack so that I could hand it over to George. Mat had disappeared, and my hunch is that he wanted George to have Mat's letters and poetry. But by then, the pack had been stolen."

Even Essie looked at me as though I'd finally lost what little mind I had left.

I kept on. "For Delgado, the pack represented a payday, a big one, and when that was gone, he must've thought it was over for himself. The backpack held a secret that Delgado hoped to cash in. The next question has to be: what secret?'"

Doctor Cleary stood up. "I have to agree with Chief López," the doctor said, "this is a waste of time, and I have too much to do to spend the rest of the night here. I'm leaving."

"I hope you don't leave, doc," I said. "I'm gonna lay out information about all of you that I think bears on Mat's disappearance. You probably want to hear what I say about you, and your family."

"You have some nerve," Cleary said. "Who the hell do you think you are?"

"I'm the private eye you didn't want looking into the mystery of your daughter's boyfriend. The guy you wouldn't talk to when I first tried to meet with you and your daughter. Your wife was so full of hate that day and wanted me to stay out of your life so much that it made me more suspicious. And I finally learned why you acted that way."

I had everyone's attention now. No one was leaving.

"What do you think you know?" Cleary said as he sat down.

"Early on, I figured that the only way for me to uncover any motive for Mat's killing was to find out all I could about the people in Mat's life . . . on the off chance that one of them hurt Mat. You all value your privacy, and me and my sister violated that in our search for the truth. I apologize, but I don't regret it." I could've used some water but I didn't want to lose the moment. "For example, I learned that Chief López left the Pueblo Police Department under a cloud. Too many complaints about heavy handedness— brutality, really. And other complaints about drinking on the job, favoritism for some people, harassment of others. The city of Pueblo paid one too many settlements, and you moved on, although your reputation among your brother cops in Pueblo seems to have not been damaged. Your pal Detective Grossman said as much. You landed this job here in Melton mainly because there weren't any alternatives. Part-time chief of a non-existent police department isn't exactly a prime job, unless you're a cop with no real future in law enforcement."

López leaped from his seat and rushed around the table to get at me. "You sonofabitch!" he shouted.

George and Bannon jumped up and intercepted the Chief. They grabbed López by the arms and wrestled him up against the wall. Both men repeatedly told the chief to calm down, to stop. He jerked himself free.

"Okay, okay," he said. "I'll leave him alone for now." He pointed at me. "But if you're trying to pin the kid's death on me, you'll regret that decision for the rest of your goddamn life. I promise you that."

"Relax, chief. You didn't do anything wrong to Mat. You might have looked harder for him, maybe you could have tried acting like real police again. You missed that Delgado had Mat's backpack. You couldn't see, or maybe you didn't want to see, that the doctor and his wife hated Mat because he dated their daughter. And you had no clue about what Mat did in Pueblo, nor did you know anything about the dangerous people in Pueblo. After all, you're only one cop, and part-time, right? But I can't say you're guilty of anything more than that."

"Quit fucking around, Corral," Bannon said. Impatience had crept into his voice. "The council knew about the chief's record. We gave him a chance, and so far, he's done a decent job. We have no complaints. Now *I'm* getting tired of this. What's your bottom line?"

I would never admit it, especially to George and Essie, but I was enjoying myself. I marched on. "I played around with other theories. It's common knowledge that George suffers from PTSD."

This time Essie shouted. "Gus! Don't. George did nothing to Mat, and you know it."

"I'm sorry, Essie. I just want everyone to be clear about my thinking. I want everyone to understand that I arrived at my conclusions only after I'd gone through every possible alternative." I waited for a response from anyone at the table, but they'd all gone quiet. "Of course George didn't do anything to Mat. He knows what I know. I've already laid it out for him. He agrees with me. Right, George?"

"That's right," George said. "I don't want it to be true, but Gus convinced me. And now we need to get justice for Mat."

"It's an interesting mix you people have here in quiet, forgotten Melton," I said. "A police chief who is decent at his job, I'll give him that, but who can get carried away questioning suspects. The town doctor and his wife . . . bigots whose daughter made the unforgivable mistake of dating a Mexican boy. A con man who duped almost everybody in the town but who only succeeded in destroying himself." I looked at George in a way that I hoped signaled that he should be ready for anything. I was getting to the end of my theatrics.

"But none of that gave me a final answer. I had my assumptions and theories, but it wasn't until a young, wounded girl talked to me about her friendship with Mat that the pieces came together. You probably saw her at the funeral. Her name is Jeannie. She looks like a mother's worst nightmare: black clothes, black makeup, skin and bones. But Mat was her friend, and the two of them talked about everything: parents, school, boyfriends, girlfriends, secrets. One thing Jeannie told me was that she always saw Mat with a backpack. He wouldn't let it out of his sight, she said. He took it everywhere."

"Good grief," Bannon interrupted. "What was so important about that damn backpack?"

"I asked her that same question. She said Mat kept his poetry in the backpack, which is what Delgado told me, too. Love poetry, she said. For his girlfriend."

"Poems?" López said. "That's what you have? I can't fucking believe it."

"Yeah, poems. And something else. Letters. Love letters from his girlfriend. Those were important to Mat. So important that he always kept the backpack close to him, although his aunt and father didn't know about it. I asked Jeannie why the letters meant so much to Mat, and she couldn't say exactly. 'He was in love,' she said. 'Isn't that enough?'"

I paused, took a deep breath, and continued. "Although people assumed Mat was broken up about his split with Yvonne Cleary, the timeline wasn't right. And it was Yvonne and *Connor* who had the serious relationship. They were off and on, off and on. I came across a picture of the two of them holding hands. There was nothing like that of Mat and Yvonne. But the clincher was when Jeannie told me that Mat had two nicknames for his girlfriend: The Cheerleader and *La Rubia*, the blonde. She mentioned that at the funeral when I pointed out Yvonne Cleary to her."

"Yvonne's not blond," Essie said. She stood up, trembling. "She was a cheerleader but . . ."

"Right, Essie. The blond cheerleader was Susan O'Brien, the cheerleading coach."

Essie immediately understood. She stared at O'Brien, clenched her hands into fists. George jumped from his chair and stood up next to Essie.

"O'Brien had an affair with my son," George said. "She took advantage of him. Her student, just a kid, and she…"

O'Brien shrieked. "No! No! It wasn't like that!" Her face turned red. "We were in love! I loved Mat! We were going to leave Melton, we had it planned. We were in love. But then he stopped. . . . It was an accident." She quit screaming.

López, Bannon and Darby stared at her in shock. They froze in their chairs.

Before any of us could react, she leaped to her feet and ran. She darted through the open door, slammed it shut behind her and kept running into the night. López scowled at me, then he turned to run after her. Cleary stood up at the same time. López stumbled into the doctor, and they tumbled to the floor. The two men fell hard and rolled, and for a minute the doctor tried to fight his way free of López. López punched the doctor, then scrambled to his feet. He ran after O'Brien.

"Hold that son of a bitch!" López shouted as he rushed out of the basement.

George and I followed the chief and caught up with him at the street. We saw nothing but the darkness that had closed around us and a faint glow from the open church basement door. No stars were visible, no moon. Black clouds shrouded the night. O'Brien had disappeared.

"Damn you, Corral," López said. "Why didn't you tell me? I could've arrested her."

"I needed to force her to say or do something that would implicate herself. I don't have the letters. Nothing. No proof. It was a gamble, but it worked. And I had nothing to lose."

"Maybe. She's running for her life now. Most likely she's headed to Pueblo or Denver. I'll go to the office and call the State Patrol, issue a BOLO on her. Then I need to talk with you. Understand?"

"Sure. No problem."

We returned to the church basement hall, where Leroy Bannon and Joe Darby watched Doctor Cleary. The doctor sat hunched over the table. He moaned and blubbered but he didn't deny George's accusations that he'd agreed to pay Delgado's blackmail money and that he and Werm helped O'Brien cover up the murder of Mat.

"It was a misunderstanding, an accident," was the most he could say.

"Is she gone?" Essie asked.

"Yeah. López is hunting for her. He'll get more cops to bring her in."

"I think I know where she's going," Essie said.

"The bluffs?" George asked.

"That'd be my guess," I said.

"Let's go get the bitch," Essie said.

"You can't, Essie," Bannon said. "It's too dangerous. López can handle this."

"I'll be all right, Leroy," Essie said. "I have to do this. For Mat. Just make sure that the doctor doesn't go anywhere."

Bannon backed off, then hugged her.

Bannon and Joe Darby agreed that they would guard the doctor until López returned to formally arrest him. The three of us—Essie, George, and me—climbed aboard my pickup and we sped into the night.

Twenty-six

In the dark pickup cab on the way to the Dead Snake Bluffs, I told Essie the same things I'd told George before the meeting.

"The only one who knew about the letters was Delgado, and he tried to blackmail O'Brien. He banked heavily on the letters. O'Brien stole the backpack from him, most likely when he passed out from too much booze or drugs, and that's when Delgado realized it was over. He couldn't even pull a con on a predatory high school teacher."

"Mat was already dead when Delgado tried to blackmail O'Brien," Essie whispered.

"Yes. Delgado didn't know that. He was playing a more dangerous game than he bargained for."

We bounced in the cab as my truck raced across the sandy prairie.

"Where does Werm fit into all of this?" Essie asked. "He knew the truth?"

"Werm and the doctor. You wouldn't think so, but they're old friends. They helped O'Brien cover up what she did. Cleary did it because she's his niece, and he'd do anything to protect the family name from scandal. Even if it meant paying Delgado. He pulled her out of a jam from her previous school. He was willing to do it again. He hated Mat anyway, because of his daughter. Werm probably owes Cleary a favor or two, maybe from years ago. Skeletons in the family closet. They buried Mat at the bluffs. Werm must've threatened Delgado to keep quiet about the poems and letters. Delgado lost it completely and he tried to kill Werm."

"But . . ." She paused. "None of this explains why O'Brien killed Mat. That is what happened, right?"

"Yes. I think Mat left the letters, the backpack, with Delgado because he was ending the affair. For whatever reason, he was finished with the teacher and he was moving on. I think he was planning to escape for good out of Melton. He'd outgrown his hometown and realized how wrong his affair with O'Brien was. The letters and poetry were important to him, no matter that the affair was over. He was thinking like a sentimental teenager. He left them with Delgado so he wouldn't have to give them up, then he met O'Brien, at the bluffs, where they would have privacy. It's where they usually met. Their special place."

"Christ," George cursed.

"Mat broke it off, O'Brien freaked. Maybe he told her that part of his new start meant he'd reveal what had gone on between them to you, George, or you, Essie. That would've been a disaster for her because of her history with a student at her previous job. Corrine dug that out for me. O'Brien would've been finished as a teacher."

"When we hired her, I didn't check her out," George said. "I believed the doctor that she was highly recommended, a real catch for Melton." He slapped the dashboard. "Goddamn!"

"Or she was simply a lover scorned," Essie said.

"Right," I answered. "That wouldn't surprise me."

"But what about those messages that we believed came from Mat?" Essie asked. "Was that O'Brien, too?"

"Had to be. She must've kept his phone. When she learned I was looking for Mat, she tried to throw me off."

"It didn't work," Essie said.

I didn't say anything for a few miles. They didn't need any more explanations.

"It's gonna be hard to see," I said when I turned at the sign pointing to the bluffs.

"Can't hold back the night," George said.

The next several minutes passed in silence. I thought about Mat and assumed that's what Essie and George were doing. I didn't want to think about the end of his life, nor about the sordid affair that he thought was love until it was too late. I avoided the evil, even though I chased it across the black prairie. I thought only of the kid from the yearbook, all smiles, lanky, long-haired, too smart for his own good.

"Lights!" George shouted. Up ahead, at the pinnacle of the bluffs, headlights beamed into the night sky.

I stopped the pickup and we jumped out.

"Susan!" Essie shouted. "Susan, it's over!"

I tried to keep up, but in the dark, I had no sure footing. I ran past O'Brien's idling car and used the glare from her headlights to guide me up one bluff, but as soon as I reached the top, I turned my ankle on a rock and fell face first into the sand. I grunted and struggled to my feet. I could see Essie ahead, but George had disappeared.

I limped to the edge of the bluff, where Essie stood. We were in darkness again.

"Do you see her?" Essie asked. "Or George?"

"I can't see anything."

The moon slipped away from the clouds, and for an instant the near horizon was bathed in silver light. O'Brien stood on the edge of the highest bluff.

"Susan! It's over," Essie shouted again.

We took off running towards her. She turned and looked back at us. The moon disappeared again, but just as we lost sight of the teacher, a shadow moved against her. She vanished in the blackness.

Essie and I made our way to the top.

"She jumped," Essie said. "She's at the bottom, where we found Mat. She jumped."

"Did you see . . . ?"

"I saw her jump," Essie said.

"We should try to find her."

"The only way down is to go around the bluffs," Essie said. "Get to the other side. We can't climb down in the dark. We should wait until morning. Let López deal with her."

Somebody moved behind me, and I turned immediately. George stared at me.

"I took the wrong trail," he said. "Did you see her? I lost her, goddammit!"

"She jumped," Essie said. "Here, where she killed Mat. She jumped."

She sighed, sobbed, turned her back and walked away.

"There was someone else, or something," I said. "Was that . . . ?"

"I didn't see anything," George whispered. He stared into the black abyss that hid the teacher's body. "Your eyes played tricks on you. It happens, especially at night."

"I guess you're right. Unless . . ."

"Unless what?" He tensed, then relaxed.

Even in the dark I could see the pain in his eyes and the tears on his face. I put my arm over his shoulders and scanned the night.

"You ever heard the story of Running Elk?"

Author's Note

We didn't know it was the last summer before the casual use of the word pandemic, before wearing a cloth mask became a political symbol, before the long days of solitude and longer nights of isolation. The protests and tear gas and street battles were yet to come. The election that would change everything waited in the wings. Hearts were broken, souls lost and the world too easily slipped into an unforeseen, unimagined surreality, a never-ending dream, the final stanza of an unwritten poem. We didn't know.